THE GLASS HOUSE

REBUILDING HOPE
BOOK 5

P A WILSON

Ebook ISBN: 978-1-990509-32-2
Paperback ISBN: 978-1-990509-33-9
Audio book ISBN:978-1-990509-34-6

FREE BOOK

Claim your copy of A Choice to Make when you sign up for my newsletter and get a glimpse of Lena and Brian at the end of the plagues.

1

———

"The Canadians have returned," Siren announced at dinner.

They still gathered for meals, but now it was rarely all of them. The work schedules had shifted over the last two months since New Year's, and every time they did, Beattie and Astrid's conflicted more with the rest, so they were often absent for days. Mellow still worked at the clinic, her time was taken more in the winter with the normal respiratory ailments, and the panic people still felt that this was the return of the plagues.

Lena and Siren had the more nine-to-five shifts. Still a teacher, she'd come to remember the joys and disappointments of her job. Siren had moved steadily up in Trixie's staff. Going from what was essentially an intern to running her schedule and meeting the people who found their way to Pearl Two looking for shelter. Everyone had settled into routines that felt like home. Lena found herself wondering if there were trade possibilities with Pearl Two and these mysterious Canadians. Their earlier suspicions faded as weeks passed without any hard proof.

"Was anyone surprised?" Lena asked. She passed the basket of whole wheat buns to Scott. Tik was across from her, next to Siren.

"Regular trip," he said. "I looked back, and they stop here every three or four months." He looked up at her. She was still surprised at how he'd lost the bedraggled looks of the road so quickly. Trixie had given him new clothes and beauty products to smooth out his skin again. The broken arm had healed completely a month ago.

"I like the sound of stable trade," she said. "We should try to meet them. Maybe they know what's happening on the east coast. Boats could make a big difference on the lakes and seaboard. If no one is interested in building unity, maybe trade is the first step."

"I'll see what I can do," he said. Like he was some kind of ambassador.

There were very few old men in leadership these days. The old had died at high rates. Today, most of the jobs they held were gone. No president. No need for CEOs or ambassadors, or generals, or... she didn't want to keep listing holes the plagues had torn through their lives.

"Thanks. Let's try to get everyone together soon. It's time to talk about leaving," she said. Pearl Two was getting too comfortable. The winter had been mild, and Lena wanted to get back to their purpose before it would be too hard to leave.

"I'll organize the shifts for next week," Siren said. "And I'll see if we need to give Trixie time to replace us."

"We are free to leave when we want," Tik said. "Luis is ready. We could move to him and stay there."

"Yes. That's the agreement. I just thought we might want to make it easier to keep good relations by not dropping everything." Siren's whine was back in his voice.

Lena was torn between relief that he was still young enough to act like a child, and despair that he would never truly grow up. She didn't have to waste time making him act more like an adult; he was Nicolette's problem. Siren was not joining them at the farm. He'd be back in the cult soon enough.

"It makes sense to at least try to hand over our responsibilities rather than just run," she said. "But we won't delay beyond that. It's a long way home, and we might not get there this year if we leave here too much later."

The fear that they would be snowbound and die of hypothermia rose again. It had dogged them the whole way from the farm to Portland. That and running out of food and clean water, or running into a gang of raiders, or falling ill, or getting injured. So much of it happened as they traveled east that Lena wouldn't risk it happening again.

"Are they trading anything this time?" Scott asked. "I know the west coast and east coast are completely different, but it might be nice to know what kind of things these guys value."

"I haven't seen the goods yet. In a couple of days, I should have enough information to answer that. I will be identifying possibilities for Nicolette as well," Siren said. "I am her representative, remember?"

Lena took a bite of her food to hide the grin. He was right, but he'd shown no sign of distance from Trixie, acting more as her agent than Nicolette's.

"Then we agree? Dinner in the next couple of days to plan our leaving?" Scott asked. "I'm going to be happy to get away from the foundry work. Riding all day has its down sides, but every hour I spend in that place, I'm waiting for some pile of metal to fall on me."

"Or watch it happen to someone," Tik said. "I think we should spend some time relearning our archery skills too."

"We all should," Lena said. "We'll talk to Beattie and Astrid about setting it up when we're all together."

2

The dinner happened within two days. Siren was efficient no matter that his alliances tended to shift temporarily. Mellow had set it up like an old-fashioned dinner party. Place cards, a white tablecloth, nice dishes, and two bottles of wine. Couples were seated across from each other with Siren at the head.

"This is kind of a celebration," Mellow said as she raised her glass. "We are about to leave and go exploring again. Dinner will be together every night, but not this nice."

She'd ordered the meal from the central kitchen. No one had to cook or clean. Lena let the tension in her shoulders relax, maybe not completely, but enough to enjoy the evening.

"Do we want to set a date?" Astrid asked. "We can tell Luis tomorrow. We were heading that way with supplies anyway."

The visits to Luis were important. To make sure he was still safe, and to transport supplies as they gathered them. Lena was not convinced that Trixie would agree they could take what they'd earned.

"How long?" Lena asked. "I mean, we should let Trixie know as soon as we decide."

"Two weeks?" Beattie said. "We still need to gather the last of the food. And I want to go foraging again with a group."

"She won't mind?" Lena asked. "I think Trixie believes she owns the contents of all the stores in Portland."

"True," Siren said, "but what are you looking for? I can check the list to see what's forbidden."

"What do you mean by that?" Astrid asked. Their relationship was still a wide swing from peers to antagonists.

"There are some supplies that Trixie won't let anyone touch." He looked around the table, suddenly uncomfortable. "It's not wrong. She has enough problems with the gangs. No one gets to hoard medical supplies or food. There are a couple of other things, but mostly she's brought them in, not taken them from anybody."

"So, if we find a cache of weapons, we bring them to her?" Beattie asked. "It makes sense."

"Yes. What are you thinking?" He pulled a small notebook from his pocket, and a pen. Lena still found it surprising to see him writing with a Mont Blanc special edition fountain pen in a Panama notebook, while wearing a Patek Philippe watch. But she was wearing a Rolex, and so were the others. Luxury goods just sat in the stores when everyone died.

"Watches," she said, remembering the long rides and the need to mark time. "I'm not sure Trixie will let us take these pretty ones. And we don't need all the bells and whistles anyway. Maybe some lighters with replacement fuel. Good trade items."

"Some paper and pencils," Mellow said. "I want to keep a journal. Pencils are lighter than pens."

"A whetstone, or a strop," Astrid said. "We need to keep our weapons sharp. Luis has the ones we brought here, but maybe a few knives?"

Siren wrote everything down, nodding his head in acceptance of each item.

"Muscle balm," Scott said.

"Definitely," Tik said. "We're going to ache for a few days. That homemade stuff will work. It keeps the bugs off, too."

"If I can't get the balm, I'll get the recipe," Siren said. "I'm going to add a few nice clothes. Maybe if we meet community leaders dressed better, we'll be more welcome."

"Let's not push our luck," Lena said. "I don't want her telling us no just because we ask for too much."

"We can't take our rides when we go, anyway," Astrid said. "We'll need to carry any last-minute things to Luis. Then we'll be back on horses, and Angel will carry the excess stuff."

"I think we'll be fine with this," Siren said. "If I think of anything else, I'll ask."

"So, two weeks," Lena said. "Early March. A bit soon for the weather change but not too much."

The discussion changed as they ate. Lena asked Beattie and Astrid to put together a training schedule. "For all of us," she said. "Only you kept up your conditioning. I guess it was mandatory for you since you were with the guards."

Over a dessert of apple crumble and tea, they left the planning details and talked about Pearl Two.

"It's good that some communities have found a way to thrive," Lena said. "I was beginning to think it was just us and the communities around the farm."

"Thriving is different for everyone," Mellow said. "I don't know how Trixie manages to keep people who cause trouble under control. I mean, we mostly did it because the other communities were already stable. She's on her own, surrounded by violent gangs."

"People don't raise trouble because of the threat of being kicked out," Siren said. "No one wants to go back out unless they have a home somewhere."

"Has she done that?" Lena asked. It was reasonable as a punishment. No community was strong enough yet to accommodate strongly conflicting opinions, and none would get there without different ideas. It was a balance Lena hadn't faced. The farm was small, and they mostly came at the same time.

"Not that I know," Siren said. "But I've watched her tell people to shape up or leave. It usually works."

"Speaking of leaving," Lena said, "one of my students has been absent for the last two days. Is she ill, Mellow?"

"Who?" Mellow asked.

"Ilsa Moody," Lena said. "I was going to drop by her home tomorrow."

"She's not in the clinic," Mellow said. "I guess she could be treating herself at home."

"That's not allowed," Siren said. "We need to know who's sick so we can contain any problems."

"I'll check tomorrow," Lena said. "She lives in one of the teens-only homes." It was a better name than orphanage, but that's exactly what most of the teenagers were here, and all over now: orphans.

3

A few days later, the estimate of it taking two weeks to get going seemed both too short and too long. Now that they were getting back on the journey, Lena wanted the freedom of the road, and Pearl Two's rules were getting on her nerves. The closer they got to actually leaving Trixie's community, the work involved seemed to double. Lena thanked whatever instinct told them early on to ship their stores to Luis throughout the winter. Not only could they carry the last things with them, but the route was familiar, and the risks were known.

Most of the trips outside Pearl Two's gates were carried out by Astrid or Beattie, rarely both. The only one of the group who had never gone beyond the back gate was Siren. No one pushed him to do it because he would need an escort. And for Lena, it meant the boy couldn't accidentally give Trixie the location.

She worried about Siren's closeness to the woman. He looked to strong female leaders, not that it was a problem, without any indication that they were people. They could make mistakes and poor choices just as much as a man. Perhaps his history made him that way, the scars from the beatings he received would always remind him that some people could be cruel.

They still had a week and a half before their deadline. Trixie was disappointed when Lena explained they were leaving, but didn't do anything to try to convince them to stay. She thanked them for the offer of handing off their duties, and gave her a list of the items they'd earned. Lena noted that it included everything already with Luis.

Lena had one more day at the school. She worried that the days of leisure would drag on for her. Mellow was working at the clinic right up to the minute they would leave. She insisted it was her choice, and that it would buy them a few more medical supplies. Beattie and Astrid's last shift with the guard was tomorrow; Scott and Tik were assigned to labor in the morning at the foundry.

"I've brought the pencils and paper," Siren called as he walked through the door, "and a few surprises."

Lena looked up and saw him laden with packages. Far more than Trixie's list. "Authorized?"

"Traded for," he said. "I don't want anyone coming after us because we took too much."

Along with the writing material, Siren placed watches on the table, one for each of them and a couple of spares. "I set them to the same as Trixie's. We can trade for them if we don't need them. Or you can take them back to the farm."

They were nothing fancy. It would be easy to see the dial. "Good idea. Perhaps Nicolette would like a pretty one?" Lena cupped her hand around the face and was happy to see a faint glow.

"I have her presents in my pack," Siren said.

"You did well. What's in the boxes?"

"Our backpacks are getting ratty, so I got new ones. Professional ones, lightweight and with lots of capacity, and you can clip things on the sides."

One of the differences between the shops around the farm and Portland, within a couple of days' ride at least, was the west coast outdoors culture. Camping equipment was vital for their journey and would help with extra accommodations at home if the new extensions were still waiting to be built. Lena listened as Siren explained all the compartments and attachments as if he was an expert.

"Our crossbows will probably fit in this side where the sleeping mat was supposed to go." He glowed with pride at his idea.

"I would never have thought about this. You are officially our head of supplies acquisition," Lena said.

"Cool. There's a few lanterns inside too, and a bunch of lighters with a box of extra fuel cartridges."

"What made you think of getting this?" If she'd been in an outdoors retailer, Lena would have taken all of these things. But without them being in front of her, she wasn't sure how much she'd have put on a list.

"I thought about all the times we were uncomfortable or had to do something the long and hard way because we didn't have the right tools."

Lena made a mental note to try this new outlook, remembering the times on the journey when they'd been forced to get creative. For her, solving the problem came easier than preparing for it.

"I have a bit more at the office," he said. "Compasses; we need spares. A couple of water-purifying kits and rain ponchos. They can help keep everything dry better than just jackets. I'll bring them tomorrow."

Lena sat back and took in the entire haul. It would go

into one of the new backpacks with plenty of room to spare. This time, they were better prepared with the lessons they'd learned on the way out. Food would still be a challenge. The boxes of dry goods and jerky would keep them going, but fresh food was needed to supplement the nutrition.

"Does Trixie send out regular scavenging teams?" In all the time they'd lived in Pearl Two, Lena had not given thought to how the world outside the walls worked. Trixie traded with the gangs and managed a market with nearby farms. Those actions seemed to keep a shaky balance with the gang leaders, but what Siren brought came from a shopping list. He'd traded, yes, but not for random things.

"Yes. But no one gets hurt. We... They go out in packs too big for the gangs to take on." Siren looked away as he spoke. The boy was still a very poor liar.

"Did you go with them?" Lena asked.

"Once," he said. "I wasn't invited back because they said I was dead weight. That one trip was plenty for me to get enough for Nicolette, and to learn what's there so I could ask for these kinds of things."

So, the pull outside was more about collecting pretty things. Lena decided it didn't matter. They had this pile of great supplies and no one was hurt. And Trixie wasn't charging them for it. "You did great," she said. "Was any of this from the traders from Canada?"

"No. They don't bring that kind of stuff. I mean, all the stores here are in Seattle and Vancouver and probably farther up and down. They bring things we don't have. Like metal for the foundry, dried fish, some herbs they grow. I guess stuff we have here or could make but it's too much trouble."

"Do you know what we send back? Or, I guess not 'we', Trixie."

"Those records are locked up. Is it important? I don't want to get in trouble. Not now we're going."

What could possibly be in those records to stop them leaving? "No, just curious. Come help me pack the tea we have left."

4

"It feels weird not to go to work," Tik said. "I mean, if Mellow and Siren were released, we could leave anytime after tonight."

More than a week early? Why did it seem so important to be gone?

It could be done without much effort. Beattie and Astrid were working their last shift and would be home soon. Lena had handed off all her responsibilities. Tik and Scott had just returned from their last day. Both were taking long showers to get the last of the greasy dirt from their skin. Siren was needed to do some critical tasks in the morning, but he'd already told them Trixie had picked a replacement. It did feel odd to know there was no work, as though they'd become freeloaders with no recognition of the work they'd done. Was it something in her nature, an ingrained need to be of use, or a reaction to unnoticed judgment? Thinking back to her last stroll around the neighborhood, Lena couldn't draw up any harsh looks or cut-off conversations. Perhaps it was all in her mind.

"Are you so anxious to get going?" she asked. "The

weather is holding, so we'll have no problems getting to the meeting with Luis. Is he ready to go?"

Tik looked out of the window. They'd consolidated into one house yesterday so the group would be together. "I guess it's the paranoia coming back. Maybe paranoia is the wrong word. Caution. We can't be as comfortable on the road. If I really think about it, I'm scared we won't go. That something will keep us here. If we show up at Luis's camp, we might stay there, but we'll be on our way, not just waiting to get going."

"What if we take this stuff to Luis tomorrow?" Lena asked. She understood Tik's uneasiness. While the feeling was less intense for her, she did have a niggling voice in her head that was saying it's too easy. Trixie would find a way to keep them if she could.

"If some of us go tomorrow, then we might as well wait. If Mellow can quit in the afternoon, we can just leave early. Not wait until our official date."

The afternoon would get them to Luis after dark. But Siren's supplies would help them travel at night. The bundle of 'other things' had included windup flashlights. Not powerful, but enough to keep them going when they were on foot.

'We'll talk about it tonight," Lena said. "It's like waiting for Christmas, right? The days leading up seem to take forever. I'm in if everyone can be ready."

Scott joined them and poured himself some tea. "I'm ready to go, too," he said. "The foundry is getting ready for some big event. Everything is cleaned and the machines are repaired enough for about ten percent capacity. Without power, that's about all they'll get."

"Siren said the traders brought metal," Lena said. "If Trixie is ready to produce, you're right. What are the odds she's not going to make ammunition and go out and slaughter the gangs?"

"Oh, she's going to do it," Tik said. "But not in the next day or two. We'll be long gone before that happens."

"Fingers crossed," Scott said. "I'm glad we opted for weapons that don't need bullets."

"Did you give her Da Vinci's design for the bolts?" Lena would be happy if guns just disappeared, but not everyone would be comfortable with a huge step back in the ability to kill. Too many people still thought a handgun or a semi-automatic would be their best protection. If they could get ammo, the world would fall deeper into violence.

"I gave it to the foundry manager. She wasn't exactly excited, but she said thanks and put them in a drawer," Scott said.

5

———

I t was lunchtime and Siren still hadn't come back from his last-minute tasks. Lena suspected that Trixie was holding him as long as she could. Maybe trying to get him to stay behind. She wouldn't know the hold Nicolette had on the boy. But Siren might be having trouble saying no to any requests she made. His absence made her surer they should follow Tik's suggestion and leave today.

"I'm going to look for him," she told Scott. "We can't let her control when we head out. And I'm not going without him."

"Mellow sent a message. She'll put in a couple more hours and then come home. I saw Beattie and Astrid heading toward the guards' stable. I expect them any time."

In a couple of hours, they could be gone from Pearl Two and all these last-minute complications. Yes, half the group didn't know they'd been talking about what was feeling more like escaping today, but she couldn't just sit around waiting. It would be dark soon after they left, but Lena's fear of being stuck was getting stronger every moment. She couldn't ignore it.

"Get everything ready," she said. "Astrid and Beattie should clean up when they get back. Use up the last of the supplies to make a quick meal."

"Don't be long," Scott said as he pulled her into a hug.

"As fast as I can."

The walk to the house Trixie used as a kind-of town hall took ten minutes, all of which Lena used to talk herself off the edge. Yelling at Trixie would accomplish nothing. Or to be more precise, nothing good.

The door was open, not unusual. Trixie liked to have an approachable reputation. Whether she was or not.

Lena stepped inside expecting to see Siren doing some make-work task. Trixie was behind her desk, a teenage girl with a shaved head and an old scar running from her jaw down below her neckline was taking instructions down on a Moleskine.

"Hello," Lena said. She felt like an idiot, but there was no polite way to break into the conversation. And she wasn't about to stand there waiting to be noticed.

"Lena," Trixie said. Her usual welcoming smile was absent. "I thought you would be gone by now."

How did she know we were leaving early? Lena forced the question to stay inside. "We'll head out as soon as Siren joins us. I thought he only had an hour of work for you."

Trixie's eyes narrowed, and the girl stepped back carefully.

"Jolie? Didn't you do as I asked and go to Lena about Siren?"

The girl's hands shook and she tightened her body. "I was just going," she said. "I thought it was more important to listen to your instructions."

Was Trixie causing this terror? Or was this something

Jolie brought with her to Pearl Two? Lena reminded herself she didn't need to know.

"It's okay," Lena said. "I'm sure you've been busy learning the job. I'm here now, that saves you the trip."

Trixie nodded to the girl. "Go ahead. Let's see how well you pass on information."

No words of comfort. Lena reminded herself again she was leaving, and she didn't know the story behind Jolie's reaction. Trixie could be saving her from a horrible past.

"Siren didn't come to work," she said. Her eyes flicked to Trixie. "One of the guards told us he went into the city. He was getting more things for you to take."

"Thank you, Jolie. That was perfect. Go take the list of duty assignments to the various leaders."

The girl started to curtsy but stopped herself. "Yes. Thank you."

She dashed out of the room.

"Not everyone is as... stable as Siren," Trixie said. "She's been through some bad shit. It's going to take a while for her to get okay with the work, maybe never competent, but I've worked with damaged goods before."

"A kind word might help." Lena immediately regretted the words.

"The man who cut her and left her to die was kind to her up to the point she refused to sleep with him." Trixie looked in the direction Jolie left. "Too soon to do anything but give her tasks she can do and build up a bit of confidence."

"Sorry, I don't know her story and you do. I don't know what Siren would go into Portland to get. I'll check with the guards to see what they think."

"Good idea. If I don't see you before you go, good luck."

Lena didn't believe a word of the story Jolie told. She'd recited the facts and looked to Trixie to make sure she had it right. Siren's words rang in her ears. He would never have gone into the city even with an escort. And there was nothing they needed that would be so dire he'd risk it.

Not buying the story wasn't enough to help her find the boy. Siren could be in real trouble. The guards might have the same script, but she could ask more specific questions. If they didn't know exactly what Siren was looking for, they weren't doing their job.

That was the second thing. First, she wasn't going to give Trixie time to mess with the others. It felt like Liberty all over again. One of their group missing when they were about to leave. But this time, there was no open space or secret back door. She took a long slow inhale and exhale to calm her fears.

When she felt grounded, Lena glanced back at the house to see if she was being observed. There was no sign, but plenty of people around who could run to Trixie with information.

She headed back to the place she'd called home for five months. No one was going to stick around. She would find out what happened to Siren. Then, from outside the walls, they would find a way to rescue him.

At the house, Lena passed on her worries. Mellow walked in just as she was finishing. "I'm going to talk to the guards at the front gate," Lena said.

"We're going with you," Astrid said. "If you believe them, then you'll need an escort."

"I doubt they'll be able to convince me," Lena said. "There is no way Siren would go past the walls without protection. He told me that yesterday."

"Eat," Mellow said, pushing a ham sandwich into Lena's hand. "This is the last of food. You aren't going anywhere alone. So, take a breath and let's form a plan."

"There's no time," Lena said. She took a bite of the sandwich because wasting food was criminal when you went on the roads these days. Her stomach rebelled for a second but then settled. Starving wasn't going to help the boy. "If Siren is gone, we need to go after him right away."

Mellow handed her a glass of water. Ignoring Lena's words, she pointed to a chair. Lena obeyed and took another bite.

"Where has he gone?" Tik asked. "Running in circles isn't the best way to use our time."

Lena swallowed and waited. Somehow, she'd been feeling the need to convince the others that Siren wouldn't do what Trixie said. But there was no pushback, at least not where she expected. They believed her but wanted to avoid the complications of just chasing after clues.

"We do need to ask the guards," Astrid said. "He's impulsive sometimes. Not smart about risks. If he thought it was important, and he could be fast... "

Like Astrid had been when they first met. Lena kept the thought inside and finished the sandwich to keep from offering ideas that came from the fear he was slipping away.

"I can do it," Beattie said. "It'll be better coming from someone with the same experience. I'm embarrassed to say a few of the guards think of citizens as a burden."

"Yeah, it's like they don't remember what you contribute." Astrid didn't notice her choice of words.

Did the choice of 'you' mean she wasn't one of people contributing? That regardless of how she disagreed with the complainers, she'd set up a them-and-us barrier in her own mind? Lena hoped it would fade as they returned to their travels. Otherwise, the journey would be filled with bickering and hard feelings.

"Okay, if Beattie is convinced that he's out there, someone goes after him," Scott said.

"That will be us," Beattie said. "Me and Astrid. We know the risks, and we've been out dozens of times."

Lena let them talk. Until everything was out, she couldn't decide on the best plan. On the one hand, she was going to send everyone to Luis and search for Siren alone. On the other, she knew how stupid that was.

"And if we don't believe what anyone says?" Tik asked. "How do we find the truth?"

"He wouldn't go without telling us," Astrid said with no trace of doubt. "Not voluntarily. He'd want us to know he wasn't scared to do the dangerous things."

"And give us a chance to talk him out of it," Tik said.

"He didn't tell anyone about the things he brought yesterday," Lena said. "He can keep a secret."

"Fine," Astrid said. "I'll just say it. He's too much of a coward to go into the city. He doesn't know how to use weapons. He won't have access to a gun or bullets. He's scared, and smart. If he wanted something, he would bargain for it like he did with all that stuff."

"Some of us should go now," Lena said. The discussion was going in circles. No one argued that Siren would have done what Trixie told her. It was odd that Trixie even bothered. "Whatever happened, that woman knows."

"Trixie?" Beattie said.

"Yes. Her new assistant is terrified. I can't be sure Trixie is responsible, but the girl was a bad liar. And Trixie knew it when she told her to deliver the message."

"Do you think she knows the truth?" Mellow asked. "The girl?"

It was hard to tell. Terror stripped away any appearance of intelligence in abuse victims. A defense against further damage. And she didn't have to be smart to know what happened, just terrified enough not to talk.

"Maybe," Lena said. "I don't think we can go ask her."

"We can, but you mean she won't tell us," Astrid said. "Fine."

"If we're going to talk to the guards, we should go now," Beattie said. "Half an hour? We'll come back no matter what we learn. No one acts without reporting in, right?"

"Yes. But Scott, Tik and Mellow should head to Luis now. Take as much as you can manage." Lena wasn't going to let everyone put themselves at risk.

"The more of us looking, the faster we can find him," Scott said.

"We split up," Lena said. "If we don't join you at the camp within a day, you can come back and rescue us. But if we're all in here, we're all available for Trixie to take."

Beattie pulled Astrid to the door. "Figure it out while we're gone."

"I'm not leaving you here," Scott said. "If she's taken Siren, she's dangerous."

"That's exactly why you need to go," Lena said. "Look, Tik and Mellow are okay with leaving."

"No, we're not okay," Tik said. "We just understand the logic. I think you should have split up those two so we had a trained fighter here and outside, but I get it."

"Tik and Mellow aren't..." Scott threw up his hands. "How can you tell me to leave you here in danger? I love you."

"I know. I'm keeping both Beattie and Astrid because you want me protected. You and Tik can fight, too. We all can, thanks to our training."

He stared at her for a long moment and then deflated. "Fine. We will talk about this when we're far from here. You had better be at the camp by midday tomorrow."

He kissed her cheek and then shouldered the pack Tik held out.

Lena stood at the door watching until they were out of sight. Beattie and Astrid would be back any minute. She closed the door and returned to check her pack.

"He's gone."

The voice startled Lena into dropping her backpack. She

looked up, and in the shadow of the living room stood Jolie, hugging her arms close around her body.

"Where?" Lena asked. "Are you okay? Has someone hurt you?"

"Yeah, but not lately. I'm better off here. No one will want to pay for me like the others. Not now I'm ugly." She pointed to the scar. "I tried to run away. They caught me. Now I'm here."

Her heart broke at the brutal acceptance Jolie showed. No one should be that beaten down. "So, nothing Trixie said was true?" Lena tried to assess Jolie's ability to take on a journey, and then stopped herself. She couldn't take in every vulnerable person they met. And Jolie hadn't asked.

"I'm safe here," Jolie repeated. "I'll find a way to fit in. Those guys with the boat? They took him. I mean. They bought him. She got me and a ton of that corrugated metal. They're heading up to Vancouver."

Trixie was working with the people traffickers? The same ones who'd taken Astrid from Liberty, or were there multiple roaming gangs along the old border taking kids for sale?

"Are you sure you're going to be okay here?" Lena couldn't just leave Jolie to be used as a... whatever Trixie wanted.

"I'll be fine. Maybe not fine, I guess. Safe if I do what she wants. I'll play stupid as long as I can. But I'll leave if she tries anything."

The girl had backbone. Lena had fallen for the same ploy as Trixie. She should have known no one survived without skills. And in truth, Jolie had moved from a very bad situation to a bad one. If she kept her wits, she'd move on to a safe place soon.

Footsteps on the front stairs made Jolie jump. "I can't be

seen." She was through the back door and gone before Astrid walked into the living room.

"We got nothing," she said. "They were all lying, and we couldn't get past it."

Beattie shut the door and joined them. "Same script. They didn't even blink when we told them he would never risk going into the city."

Lena picked up her pack. "He's on that ship," she said. "Trixie is giving them people in exchange for goods."

7

I t was dark before Lena and her companions joined the rest of the group. The camp was comfortable because Luis had months to make it more like a residence than a temporary shelter. He'd set up storage places on the ground floor of an old hotel, and a stable for the horses in a conference room. They met in the kitchen of what had been the restaurant as soon as everyone dropped their backpacks.

Walking for a few hours had been hard. The weight of supplies they carried and the lack of exercise over the winter meant their stamina was almost nonexistent. What would they do with the extra supplies? Angel wouldn't be able to carry everything. Traveling for the first few days or weeks was going to be hard on their bodies, but she had no intention of leaving anything here while they went after Siren. When they freed him, Lena was not coming anywhere near Portland.

"We'll use Olive as a pack until we get Siren back," Luis said as if he'd read her mind. "We've been organizing since Tik, Scott, and Mellow got here."

"So, we go in the morning?" Lena asked. "First light?"

"Let's hope they aren't running straight for Vancouver," Scott said. "We have to backtrack and avoid Portland."

They'd placed a map on the counter. Lena bent over it to try to find a route that wouldn't take them too far inland.

"Eat first," Luis said. "We need to be in good shape when we head out. Eat, plan, rest."

As if I'll sleep, Lena thought.

"The ship is stuck going upriver and then to the coast," Scott said. "We can shortcut all the way up by going off-road. Good horse country if we bypass the official routes. And if they are still trading, they'll need to stop here and there. Every hour they're docked gets us closer to their location."

The good news gave Lena a moment of optimism. They would catch the boat. They would get Siren away from the traders. And they would head south. The weather would hold. Then, a flood of the hazards filled her mind, drowning out the hope.

"Food?" she asked, hoping her feelings came from hunger and exhaustion.

"Sit," Luis said. "I've been experimenting. The kitchen was fully stocked. I guess no one found it. The fresh stuff must have been taken right at the start, so I was spared the stink and vermin."

He'd set a table in the restaurant with a white tablecloth, silver cutlery, and crystal wine glasses. Three bottles of red were open and placed at each end and the middle of the table. Luis had been expecting a celebration, not a hurried meal.

The others joined her and then Luis came in with bowls of soup. Beans in a vegetable broth with spices Lena hadn't tasted for a while.

"Sorry it's just crackers to go with," Luis said. "I have a surprise for later."

The dinner ended up being a happy occasion, mostly due to the wine. Luis opened more as the bottles emptied. He kept moving the discussion back to the journey after the rescue. "There is no point in talking about the dangers we might face while we've got this feast in front of us," he said. "Enjoy this and we can return to the plan over my little surprise."

The soup was followed by a plate of chicken and rice. "It's not real Cuban food," Luis said. "The spices I needed were missing, and it's canned chicken. But it's close to *arroz con pollo*."

After the plates were cleared, Luis showed them their rooms and told them to clean up and come back to the kitchen for planning.

The surprise was blown as Lena approached the kitchen. The aroma lured her in: Coffee?

Luis had placed espresso cups in a line and stood grinning with a large *Bialetti* in his hand.

"Oh my god," Lena said. "Is there more? Can we pack it?"

"I ground the last for tonight. Maybe one or two more pots," Luis said. "It's better that way. Making coffee on a fire is never going to be as good. Better we remember it here."

She took the first sip. "Heaven."

When everyone was settled, they stood over the map. The river was clearly marked. "See how it wanders?" Tik said. "They'll hit the ocean at Long Beach. That's our first opportunity to act."

"It looks like we can do a straight ride," Mellow said. "Camp for a few hours. Get there in two days if we push?"

"If they go straight through, that's when they get there." Scott pointed at the location. "They'll go up to the coast for a while. We can probably see them from the shore. They'll know how to avoid the rocks, but getting out of sight of land will be dangerous."

"Next place is here?" Lena pointed to Blaine.

"Unless they're going around to the port in Vancouver directly," Luis said. "If it was me, I'd stick with a smaller port. Blaine doesn't have a real one, but plenty of places to anchor and take a small boat in. Two days later, you're in Vancouver, faster if you push it with a load of captives, and no one knows where your ship is."

"And why wouldn't they go around and dock in Vancouver?" Mellow asked. "If it's got a real port."

"Because someone else might have control of it," Tik said. "Or they're taking a few things off the shipment. Skimming is pretty normal in gangs. They need a place and time to drop a few people and maybe some crates."

"So, we have a plan," Lena said. "Get some sleep, we're out of here at first light."

8

T he ride was easier than Lena expected. The snow stayed away. The horses enjoyed the chance to stretch into a gallop as they crossed country. If it wasn't for the reality of their mission, Lena would have been taking in the rush of adrenalin and the view of trees, streams and gentle hills. But the fear Siren was gone forever cast a grayness on the world.

Now they were lying on the gravel and tar roof of a museum in Astoria, searching for signs of the ship. Lena couldn't see a way for them to do anything about rescuing Siren. The ship would sail through and out into the Pacific. No narrows or real places for the ship to dock. No small boats to use if the ship dropped anchor.

They'd stopped in Astoria because going farther would leave them with a long backtrack to continue north if they wanted to confirm the ship's route. Here they could watch the ship pass, and with any luck, see Siren on deck. Lena hoped sight of him would relieve some of the guilt she felt by letting him get taken.

"We have time to get to Blaine ahead of them," Beattie

whispered. "If Luis is right, they'll put down an anchor and we'll have a chance to board. If not, they'll be on land to get to Vancouver, and we'll have days to act."

"I know we can't worry about the other side of that coin. That we've guessed wrong, or that they lied about Vancouver and are headed south. That Jolie lied and Siren is still in Pearl Two." She stopped talking.

"Yep," Beattie said. "It's hard to stop that kind of thinking. Look at it this way. If we don't see the ship in the next couple of days, then we try something else. They can't have gotten here before us."

"I know. They need more wind than we have. Even if they went Viking and made the captives row, they'd still take four or five days to get here with the tides. I wish we'd seen the ship when it was in Portland, if only so we'd know it by sight."

"Wishes only make you unhappy," Astrid said. "They never come true."

At least they didn't have to stay here on the roof for the whole time. The horses were downstairs in the main hall, their camp was in one of the side offices. Everyone worked assigned shifts to watch, and no one believed the ship would try to come through in the dark. The passage was too narrow where it opened to the Pacific.

"It's now that I wish we'd brought the coffee," Lena said.

"He brought the *Bialetti*," Astrid said. "Something about finding beans on the way up?"

"Now you tell me after saying wishes were useless." Lena chuckled and hoped anyway, one tiny shred of positivity to help her make it through the waiting.

"Your shift is over," Beattie said. "Scott should be ready."

The shifts were staggered so that there were always fresh eyes looking across the water. Lena struggled up from her position. The bulk of the cold weather gear made it hard to stand. "See you in a couple of hours."

Their camp inside the museum was dry and warm. Having the horses nearby helped keep the air from getting frigid. The smell of the animals was a downside, but worth it. Setting fires didn't always work inside, not enough ventilation in most places, and an intact roof was better than one with holes. Smoke gave away their position, so setting a fire was often too much of a risk. Lena huddled down in a corner with the others and wrapped her hands around a mug of tea.

"Are you sure we couldn't miss them?" she asked.

"Look, I know they had a two-day start on us," Tik said. "But they need wind to move at any speed, and the tide would be against them half the time. We can ride for a while in the dark, but they can't. They are a day behind us at best."

The logic was sound, but without proof, Lena couldn't relax. "From here, is it possible to keep them in sight?" The ship would be off the coast, and from what she remembered, only a few roads stayed close to the water all the way up.

"If the timing works," Luis said. "Not all the time, and we want to arrive well ahead of them. If they dock here in the evening, we can verify and then head out. By the time they round the point, we can be near the coast. Then it depends."

"And if they aren't the only ship on the water, we might not be able to pick out the right one," Mellow said.

"I guess I can try patience," she said. "Or, maybe we can go look around the town?"

"Let's be careful," Luis said. "Just because we haven't seen anyone doesn't mean it's abandoned."

Lena couldn't just sit and wait. Even an hour in the town would help. "Anyone want to come?"

"Me," Tik said. "I'm on duty in a couple of hours."

"Then we'll make it fast." Lena stood and gathered an empty sack to hold whatever they found. She took her bow and a handful of bolts for protection if they couldn't run. Tik joined her at the door, they zipped their jackets and slid out.

The streets were empty. But Portland had seemed empty too, until it wasn't.

"We should work the streets off our path in to get new information," Tik said. He looked up at the cloudy sky. "Weather should hold, and I don't smell snow."

"Rain is just as bad," Lena said. She turned the corner and walked close to the storefronts a block away from the museum.

The places near their camp were all vandalized, any supplies inside would have been taken by the scavengers or by animals. She checked quickly for evidence of recent human activity. There was none. Towns like this had fallen pretty fast during the plagues. Lots of death and very little in the way of options for the survivors. A day's ride or walk would have put them in farm country. These days, anyone running a farm needed labor.

"Drugstore on the next block," Tik whispered. "Diner, too."

Both were in the same condition as the other stores. "A few more blocks and then we go back," Lena said. The idea of staying out for an hour suddenly depressed her. "I don't think there's anything left." She hoped it was unusual. If all the towns on the route were like this, the supplies would dwindle too fast.

The business that wasn't completely empty was a craft store. Lena packed yarn and fabric into the sack along with the tools that might come in handy for all kinds of uses.

As they approached the museum again, someone gave a short sharp whistle. She looked up to see Astrid beckoning.

"It's here," she said.

Tik ran with her to the doors. They dropped the packs in the empty foyer and headed upstairs. The entire group was laying on their bellies, binoculars trained over the water.

Astrid and Beattie handed theirs to the two newcomers. "We've seen enough," Beattie said. "It's them. You need to look for yourself. We are headed down to where it's warm."

Lena lay beside Scott and trained her binoculars on the ship. She could see everything. On deck was a small crowd. Five wearing appropriate gear. The remainder in street clothes and light jackets.

The five stood on the higher deck and were ordering the others to action. As she watched, the sails loosened and dropped. The ship's forward motion stopped, forcing her to refocus.

On the deck, at the front, two people were manhandling the anchor over the side. Ilsa Moody, the girl who went missing from Pearl Two, and Siren.

Following the ship was more difficult than Lena hoped. They didn't leave right after seeing their people on board because Lena wanted to make sure they turned north when out on the Pacific. Her anxiety didn't diminish after confirming they had the right ship and their assumptions were correct; it increased.

"Not all the way," she argued when Beattie said they were wasting time continually turning for the coast. "Just enough to be sure they are headed in the right direction."

"That ship won't turn around," Beattie said. "We need to get ahead of it so we're ready to board as soon as they dock or drop anchor."

Lena knew Beattie was right. The ship wasn't going to suddenly veer off toward Russia or Japan. There was no way the sailors were good enough at navigating without GPS. The Pacific was full of dangers. They might not go to Blaine, and they might not stop in Vancouver. There were ports farther north that made sense, too. Vancouver would still have people. Why would they need to steal kids? North was

Prince Rupert and Alaska. People were scarce up there even before the plagues.

"The weather will keep them here," Luis said. "The farther north, the worse it will get. If they are trading up there, smaller boats or land travel make more sense."

She wasn't going to win. Mostly because her internal argument was the same as the external one. She knew they were probably right about where the ship would stop. She knew they could move closer to the ocean later in the journey.

"One more day?" she said. "No. I'll make do with just today. We head inland tomorrow. I'll just deal with it."

"Okay, that puts us at Long Beach. After that, we head inland, skirt Seattle and then west again." Scott pointed to the route on the map. "We can't go beyond that, or we'll have to find a boat to cross back to the mainland and leave the horses behind. We know their pace. It's going to be at least four more days before they get to Blaine. At Bellingham, we'll find them and track their progress if you really need to. I say we go straight to Blaine."

It all made sense, and going inland gave them way more options for camping. "It's three days for us," she said. "Go as late as we can, get up early. No stopping during the day."

"Unless we get held up by a freak snowstorm," Tik said. "We know how to deal with bandits, and we'll avoid the larger towns."

"A storm will delay the ship too," Mellow said. "Lena, we have to trust what we know."

"I do. And I have no idea why I'm so anxious. Siren and Ilsa looked healthy. It's to the traders' benefit to keep them that way. I just... I don't know."

"It's Trixie," Scott said. "Lena, we all feel like there's a big bad thing heading our way. We all trusted that Pearl Two was a safe place. That Trixie was doing the right thing. We were wrong. I know I feel like I can't trust my instincts anymore."

"She was doing the right thing," Astrid said. "The right thing for her. I don't know how many people in Pearl Two know the truth. You can't let her lies rule you."

It was more than Trixie; Lena knew it was all the little betrayals and challenges up to this point. Even the few places where they'd felt safe had secrets. And her vision of a country allied against this kind of horror was dying a slow death. Would it matter if they saw the ship tomorrow? It was behind them right now. A long way from shore, and every time they stopped to look, they lost a bit of their lead.

"Okay, we go now," she said. "Get to Blaine as fast as we can. Give ourselves a bit of time to scout the town. If they are dropping anchor, then someone might be meeting them with supplies or more people."

THE CLOUD of doubt followed Lena the entire journey to Blaine, Washington. No one had challenged them, but they had stayed off the main roads, sticking to open country as much as possible. Now they were on a point that allowed them to look south. Blaine was barely a town, and tomorrow, they would reconnoiter for hiding places, occupants, and boats to take them out for the rescue.

It was late afternoon, and the ship was nowhere in sight. So even if it appeared in the next few minutes, the traders would be stuck on board for the night.

"There," Astrid whispered.

Lena followed her direction and saw the mast above the trees that hid the shore just north of the marina.

The traders made faster progress than expected. And they were close enough to shore that a small boat could reach them easily. She watched for ten minutes, according to her watch. They were anchored for the night. There was no safe place to offload the cargo until morning.

"We have time to get to the marina," Scott whispered. "Tik and Beattie can check for people and join us before dark."

For the first time since she knew Siren wasn't meeting them in Pearl Two, Lena felt the weight of her worries lift.

The marina was a problem. Far from the orderly rows of boats tied up along a dock, there were empty spots with only the top of the mast showing a boat had sunk. The dock itself was rotting in places, and someone had cut the lines, allowing five boats to float into the entrance, which had effectively blocked passage.

"How are they planning to get people off the ship?" Mellow asked. "You think they're just stopping here for the night? Or to pick up some more cargo?"

"We won't know until we look closer," Scott said, "and when we know the situation in town. This could all be camouflage."

It looked real enough to Lena, but there were other docks and a launch ramp at the far end. As Scott said, a closer look might reveal a way to get out there and take back the captives.

They carefully scouted each dock, keeping an eye out for any sign of the traders approaching by boat. Once they came into sight, the rescuers would have no way of hiding their activities.

"Astrid's back," Mellow whispered.

The girl was standing on the road beside the marina,

looking for them through sunglasses she hadn't owned an hour ago.

Lena signaled for everyone to join her.

"There's no one here," Astrid said. "Beattie is on her way. We found evidence that we're right. There's horses stabled just outside of town. A wagon and fucking shackles."

10

Beattie met them halfway back to the town and redirected them. "There's another dock," she said. "All clear and a few boats. They'll notice if we take one."

"Then we need to make a way out of the one we just came from," Mellow said. "We should check to see if any have fuel. I don't know how we'll get out, otherwise."

"If those boats aren't anchored, we can push them aside easily," Tik said.

"I think we do it now," Lena said. "We can't when they get here. And it will be dark soon, which will hinder us as much as them."

An hour later, Lena scrambled onto the last boat that still floated at the end of the longest dock. It was big enough that they would be able to take ten or more people. So far, none of the boats had started, either no fuel or the fuel was no longer any good.

Scott joined her on the deck and turned to look toward the sea. "Those boats are floating around too much to be anchored."

"We might have to swim out to rescue them. Or paddle, if we can find oars." Lena lifted a net covering from the center of the deck and grinned. "If this one starts, we're good to go, right?"

"As far as the entrance," he said. "We'll have to wait out there until it's safe to move closer."

She looked up at the sky. The clouds were lifting and thinning. She pulled the whole netting off and pointed.

"Solar? Get everyone here." He slipped below deck to check the controls.

Lena gave the low whistle that they'd agreed on as a signal and then waited for the others to join her.

Scott poked his head up and called them inside ten minutes later. "Leave the netting off. An hour of light will charge us enough to leave. Those batteries have been topping up every day."

Inside, Scott pointed to the glowing dials on the dash-board. "There's been enough light that the batteries are good enough for a short trip. The net must be designed to protect without completely blocking the sun."

"Noise?" Lena asked. "That was our next problem, the sneak factor."

"You had electric vehicles before, right?" Tik said. "How did they sound?"

"The manufacturers were forced to add noise as a safety factor." If someone came up with a way to charge the electric cars, they'd have transportation.

"We'll see," Scott said. "Anyone know how to drive one of these things?"

"You steer it like a car," Luis said. "Just avoid rocks, and don't get stuck in an eddy. We all going?"

An hour later, in the dimming light, Luis untied the

lines, and Scott steered the boat slowly through the obstructions out past the entrance to the bay.

Tik and Mellow stayed behind to protect their horses and supplies. Any captives needing medical attention would need to wait until everyone was safe.

The slow progress out to the sound was more painful than the entire ride to Blaine. Lena was happy to leave the steering to Scott, with Luis helping. If she'd been in charge, they would have been discovered immediately because she would be at full throttle and bashing into any obstacle.

The ship's anchor splashed into the water just as they came into view. Scott cut the engines. No matter how quiet they were, anyone on board would be suspicious of an approaching boat.

It was getting dark fast. The break in the clouds was closing as night fell. If the ship didn't put out lights, they wouldn't be able to locate it soon.

"Patience," Astrid whispered. "We have all the time in the world. If no one leaves tonight, they'll do it tomorrow. But there's no reason for them to stay aboard."

"Tomorrow in daylight it will be a fight," Lena whispered back.

"It will be a fight anyway." Beattie crouched beside them. "Look, lights are going on."

Lena's plan counted on some of the traders going ashore, but it wasn't the only solution. "Give them a bit to see if anyone leaves," she said. "If not, we can handle them as long as they don't see us coming."

"Yes, we can," Astrid said.

Lena checked her watch and counted out a half hour. Just as she was going to tell Scott to go ahead, a louder splash sounded, a boat hitting the water on the far side of the ship.

Then voices carried across to the waiting rescuers. Nothing Lena could make out, but male voices. And it didn't sound like orders. Whoever was on the smaller vessel was in a good mood, chatting and the occasional burst of laughter reached them.

"We're not going to see them leave," Luis said. "Just a small gap after they pass the ship, then hidden by the rocks."

"We go as soon as they pass the gap," Scott said. "I can hold the boat near the anchor chain. You'll be vulnerable until you get up if anyone is watching from shore."

"I'm counting on there being a lifeboat or something we can lower," Lena said. "If not, the captives will have to jump."

"Don't waste time with a lifeboat," Scott said. "Send them down the anchor chain, or a jump. Noise won't matter so much then."

He looked across and then hurried back to the dials and steering wheel. Lena felt a shift when the boat moved. Not too fast, but directly for the chain. She scanned the upper rail of the ship. No one was watching them.

Scott pulled in as close as possible and Luis took the chain, leaning his weight on it to keep it still. The boat stopped and Beattie climbed, followed by Astrid, then Lena. The metal was cold and hard to grip. A few rags of seaweed clung to Lena's fingers, and she started to feel she wouldn't make it when hands reached down and hauled her over the railing. Luis slipped over just behind her.

They were alone on the deck. Lanterns shone from the prow and the stern. Enough light to see where they were going, but low enough to keep shadows to hide their progress.

"Wait here." Astrid breathed the words into Lena's ear. "We'll check it out."

11

Astrid returned an age later. Lena kept holding her breath, waiting for the sound of a fight, or to be captured, or any one of a hundred fates that she hadn't anticipated. The battle with Newton Cole kept running in her head. The only time the people who lived at the farm took up weapons, assisted by their neighbors.

The only time she'd killed anyone.

"One guard, but he's falling asleep." Astrid glanced over her shoulder and tensed. "We can take him out, but it will make noise. Beattie says it might carry to the others on land. We move quiet."

"The captives?" If they could sneak in and out, Lena would be satisfied. By morning, the whole rescue party would be long gone, south of here. "How do we keep them quiet enough?"

"I saw Siren in the hold. No one is tied up. They look healthy. Maybe a few bruises. It looks like he fought a bit, but he learned his lesson. Ilsa is sticking to him. Don't recognize the others, but they could be from Pearl Two. I don't think anyone is going to make noise and jeopardize their freedom."

She couldn't know that. Lena tried to think through the options. Could Siren and Ilsa manage the others? Why hadn't she thought about this earlier? What if someone was injured?

"We should go now. It will only get riskier," Luis said. "Where's Beattie?"

"Picking the lock on the hatch to the hold." Astrid pointed toward the raised deck.

"How close is the guard?" Lena wouldn't hesitate in dealing with him if needed.

"Drunk, we can get by easily. It's when we come out. Beattie thinks they left only one behind because some of the captives are actually traders. People reporting on what happens when they're alone."

"Let's go," Lena said. "We came here to rescue people. We can sort out the complications later."

Astrid tapped the knife in Lena's belt sheath. "Weapons ready."

She led them at a crouching walk toward the center of the deck. What Lena thought was a barrel set to the side turned out to be Beattie waiting for them in the shadows.

The hatch to the hold was still closed, but she held up a padlock and then put it to the side.

"The guard is over there," Astrid said, pointing again.

A man sat on an office chair, a bottle on the deck next to a handgun. His chest rose and fell slowly. If they kept it silent, he wouldn't know the captives were free until they were long gone.

Beattie pointed through the grating to the people below. Siren was sitting at the foot of the ladder. The first to go up and last to go down, a protective stance she didn't expect from the boy.

Astrid nudged Lena and handed her a handkerchief, making dropping motions. Lena reached over and tried to aim for the floor at Siren's feet. The cloth hit his head instead.

He pulled it off and frowned at it before looking up. He smiled when he saw them but put his finger to his lips. Beattie gently lifted the hatch enough to prove it was open and then lowered it.

Siren nodded and moved away. In moments, people started to gather at the foot of the ladder. Beattie opened the hatch and placed the cover quietly on the deck. Lena turned her attention to the guard. If he woke now, they wouldn't get away without violence. His body moved with a deep breath and then a snore shattered the silence.

Luis slipped down the ladder and the quiet murmur of instructions drifted up. The guard grunted and then shifted his position. Lena held her breath, but he didn't wake.

The first people up were young, barely preteen. They headed to the anchor and slipped over the side one by one. Then older ones, teenagers and people who couldn't be more than early twenties. Then Ilsa, followed by Siren.

He waited with them until the rest of the captives were over the side. He looked at the guard and then back at Lena. He pointed to her knife and mouthed, "I need a weapon, too."

Lena started to shake her head, but Astrid's hand slipped between them with a throwing knife. She gave him a hard stare, which he returned. What was she saying? Lena didn't want to know. If they were planning to kill the guard, it could give the escape away for no reason but revenge.

Siren took one more look at the sleeping man and turned to where the anchor chain waited to send him to freedom.

They tiptoed across, avoiding the same ropes and barrels as before.

Siren stood back and gestured for Luis to go first.

"What the fuck is going on?" the guard called out as he stood.

Siren turned and threw his knife into the guard's throat. "He was going to raise the alarm," he said, then slipped over the side.

Astrid and Beattie stood on the deck, scanning for evidence they hadn't missed reinforcements.

"Go," Beattie said, nudging Lena. "We're right behind you."

Lena took hold of the chain and climbed over the side. On their boat, Scott was telling Siren to get below. Luis held the chain tight.

There was no sound from the ship.

Lena lowered herself hand over hand to the deck, feeling the jolt as someone got on the chain. Astrid hit the deck at the same time as Lena. The girl had jumped from halfway down.

Beattie hissed for them to move as she hung from the top, letting go as soon as they stepped back.

Luis steadied her. "Go in and settle. Scott's not sneaking back to shore." He held Lena's arm as she moved to join the others.

"What?" she asked, feeling the beginnings of adrenalin shakes.

"There's a problem. Siren confirmed Beattie's suspicions; there's a plant in the group. He doesn't know who, but the traders knew too much about what was going on in the hold at night."

"What do we do about it?" Lena asked. "I won't just leave everyone here to avoid dealing with the risk."

"I didn't mean that," Luis said. "We watch the captives, and when we find out who the mole is, we deal with them."

12

"Wait," Lena said. "We can do something more." She ran down to tell Scott to hold off on leaving. "We need to stop them, at least for a while. Can we unlatch the anchor?"

"No, the chain is tight, and we don't have the equipment to cut through the metal even if we weren't worried about the racket." He looked back and called Siren to join the conversation.

"We can reel it in," Siren said. "We felt the ship being pulled by the anchor all the time. There's enough tide to drift the ship away before the others get back."

Lena didn't want to scuttle the ship. Losing something that could be used to transport goods for trade or to explore farther seemed wrong. Even if it wasn't of use to them, surely there were people on the coast who weren't criminals.

"That will have to do," Lena said. "If the ship is drifting, it will take them longer to find out what exactly happened. The more of a head start we have, the better. I don't care if we've got a traitor in the captives. They'll have no one to report to, so no danger."

She took Siren with her to the prow of the boat where Astrid and Beattie stood guard. "Do you need help on board?"

"I'll do it," Astrid said. "We can climb up and back without a problem."

She took hold of the chain and started up before Lena could take offense at the jab. The girl was right. Lena was exhausted.

Siren waited until Astrid leaned over the railing and beckoned. Within minutes of him reaching the top, the chain was rising.

"How are they going to get back on?" Luis asked.

"We need to give them room to land in the water," Lena said.

"I'll go," Luis said. "There are some life rings up in the prow. Good thing Astrid didn't load up on weapons and Viking gear when she went up."

Lena kept watch as the anchor rose out of the water. The movement was smooth but not silent. The traders on land would know something happened if they heard it. That small boat could be sliding into view any moment. This distraction was only worth it if they got their head start.

As soon as the anchor was out of the water, the ship started to drift. The chain stopped rising and Siren was already halfway down when Lena realized the boat needed to stay in place.

"Stop," she shouted, not caring who could hear.

Siren looked up at Astrid, who was climbing down to meet him. The ship still drifted, neither would be able to drop onto the deck. She looked around the deck for something that would hold them closer. Under the life rings was a long pole with a hook on the end. She leaned out towards the chain.

It was too far. But the anchor wasn't. The hook barely held as Lena pulled, bringing the boat forward, rather than the anchor toward her.

"Now," Astrid said.

Both dropped and landed beside Lena.

"Go," she shouted as they ran to get below deck.

THE TRIP back to shore was slow as Scott maneuvered their boat between obstructions in the dark. On deck, Beattie and Astrid kept scanning the shore for evidence the trackers had found them.

"Stay on board," Beattie said after they pulled alongside the dock. "We'll do a quick check. Astrid will go to Mellow and Tik, and they can get ready to leave. We'll be stuck at a walk, but there's better ways to cover our tracks at that pace. I'll come back and help get everyone out."

Lena pulled Siren away from the crowd while they waited. "You think they can travel?"

"Are you going to bring them all with us? All the way?" He rubbed his forehead in thought.

It hadn't occurred to her that anyone but Siren would want to come with them as they crossed the continent. "It's not practical. You, maybe Ilsa, but fifteen new people, no horses, no supplies? No."

"Good. I think they'll be fine for a day, maybe two. But yes, they'll be able to travel long enough to get away. After that, you need to ask them."

He hadn't mentioned Ilsa, just lumped her in with the group. "And the plant? I can't let them betray us."

"I don't know who it is," he said. "I can try to find out as we run. But maybe Luis and I can watch to make sure no one is setting a trail?"

Lena's assurance that they'd be safe with the spy because they were isolated disappeared. Of course they could leave markers for the traders to follow. "It shouldn't matter," she said, trying to believe her own statement. "We'll be long separated by the time those guys find us. Even with a trail, they'll be hours behind."

He didn't look like he agreed, but there was nothing she could do about it. If she had any clue who the spy was, let alone proof, she would leave them on the ship, tied up, needing rescue. Making for a longer delay before anyone would be on their trail.

"The kids? Will they need breaks?" She wanted to be as prepared as possible, even knowing that a plan was worthless when they got going.

"They kept us fit and well fed. More valuable that way. I heard them say that's why they fattened cattle in the old days. More weight, more money." He shrugged as if it meant nothing to him.

"I'm sorry," Lena said.

"It's not the worst I've heard," he said. "You know, I've been in the same kind of situation before, without the food and care, and I don't want to talk about it."

She wanted to point out how he'd changed. There was no pouting, no whining. He'd taken on some kind of leadership role without noticing. Whatever he decided to do, go back to Nicolette or travel, he wouldn't easily be taken again.

"Let's go," Beattie whispered as she appeared silently beside the boat. "The traders all headed back to the ship. They are idiots not to leave anyone here, but that's in our favor."

Mellow checked all the captives for injuries or any impediment to a fast walk. Anyone who would slow them down was put on a horse. Only three of the youngest were riding. No injuries, just a worry they wouldn't move fast enough.

"Was anyone in better shape?" Lena asked Mellow as they led the group toward their path south.

"Not enough to show they got special treatment," Mellow said. "Siren told me about the traitor. We'll all watch closely."

———————

13

They kept going until mid-morning, stopping just south of Ferndale, another apparently abandoned town. The entire walk, Lena waited for the sound of galloping horses. She'd expected this larger group would move slower, but the reality was frightening.

Some of the captives had been on the ship for months. They'd worked, but in short bursts. Their stamina was gone. Without them, Lena's party would be twice as far away from danger. With them, the best she could hope for was ten miles in a day.

Astrid and Beattie had taken turns scouting ahead. Lena suspected it was more about leaving the slow pace behind than an excess of caution. When Beattie returned from her last foray, she brought news of a golf course and clubhouse.

"No one there, and the doors lock, so we can defend it if we have to," she said. "You need to decide how many of our supplies you are going to share. And this is as good a place as any to have the conversation."

"We need to know their plans before we start handing out food and equipment," Lena said. "We don't talk about our next steps until they are gone, right? I don't want those traders coming after us. We've avoided violence so far. I'm not ready to start real fighting."

"No argument from me about that. You talk when we get settled in," Beattie said.

IT TOOK another hour to get to the resort, and almost another to get settled in for a rest and conversation. Now, the whole group sat in the restaurant next to the pro shop. The tables were pushed together so they could talk quietly and still be heard. Eight original members and fifteen new ones. One, at least, who couldn't be trusted.

The oldest woman of the released captives stood. She couldn't have been more than twenty. Her face wasn't yet carrying the evidence of a hard life. The clothes she'd been wearing on the ship were dusty and damp from the trek, but there was still an air of freshness and energy about her.

"My name is Trish," she said, then cleared her throat. "Sorry, we weren't allowed to talk that much. Get a little rusty."

Lena nodded at her to continue, hoping she would share their plans, and dreading it at the same time. Whoever had been passing information on about the captives would use it as ammunition.

"You should know the story," Trish said. "Your people, Siren and Ilsa, they only came on board a week ago. Maybe a bit more, we kind of lost time on the ship. These guys are part of a bigger gang. Trying to repopulate the land around the border. These ones operate all down the coast. I came from Monterey, they already had two kids on board."

"That far?" Scott asked despite the agreement that only Lena would speak. "This isn't just a few guys with a ship.

They must be affiliated with the ones who tried to take Astrid."

"Where was that?" Trish asked.

Lena wondered if they should share any details with her. The woman knew a lot about the operation. If she was so willing to talk, maybe that was proof she wasn't the mole. Or she was a very good one.

"Back east a bit," she said. "How do you know so much?"

Trish looked around the table at her companions. "They talked. Drank too much. Bragged. I don't know if they didn't think we could hear, or didn't care."

"What are your plans?" Lena asked. There was still enough daylight to get farther away. Or start on their own trek south until they felt safe stopping to plan better.

Ilsa stood and there was a little staring battle between her and Trish. Then the older woman shrugged and sat.

"We need a bit of food," she said. "Not much. We'll scavenge; there's a bunch of stores all along the highway. We'll fight if they find us. I'll be straight with you, Lena. We're going to fight back. We'll start with Trixie. When Pearl Two is in better hands, we'll move south and set the next asshole straight on the cost of selling people."

Lena turned to Siren. "Are you joining them?"

"No. I'm coming with you. Nicolette needs to know about this. Imagine what will happen if this gang finds my home."

The faster they could get away from what was rapidly turning into a gang of rebels, the better.

"Then we split here," she said. "We can spare one meal, we'll share it. Maybe a few supplies. We can't give you weapons or horses."

"We'll find them," Ilsa said. "Thanks for what you can give us. We'll be moving on after the young ones rest."

"You need to know that someone in your group was feeding information to your captors."

"We all did things that we regret to survive," Ilsa said.

"Then we agree. A meal, and then you're on your own." Lena stood and shook Ilsa's hand. "Good luck."

"We passed a few of those malls on the highway on the way down," Astrid said. "I didn't see any signs of life. I could go, maybe Beattie and Tik could come. We can find these guys some supplies?"

"Okay," Lena said. "Be fast and safe."

"I'm coming with you," Ilsa said. "We need to know how to do it. Scavenge safely."

"You have two hours. Eat in the saddle, we'll see what's here. Maybe a set of clubs that can be used as weapons."

THE GOLF CLUB had been bypassed by scavengers, not all of them would come this far from the main road. There were rain clothes, tee shirts, and other golfing outfits available in all sizes. What equipment they found would be useless for camping, and the golf clubs were all gone. Likely taken by their own members during the final waves of the plagues.

"It's going to take you weeks to get to Portland," Lena said to Trish, who'd joined her.

"We'll get there eventually," Trish said. "Even if we get there in a couple of days, we'll have to find shelter. It's probably going to rain until April, right?"

"I'm not from here," Lena said. "That is what people say, but I don't know how much truth there is to it."

"We'll do a lot of scouting. You said you came from the east, right?"

"We didn't travel this far north," Lena said. She changed the subject. "When you search through a place like this, you need to look everywhere, not just the obvious places." She opened a door that Trish had walked past. Inside was a large janitor's closet. "You can use the broom handle as a staff."

Trish leaned inside and pulled out two mops and the broom. "These too. I'll get someone back here later."

"Didn't you need to do this where you came from?"

"I was part of a larger community. Sounds pretty much like this Pearl Two. We had people who scavenged, but I wasn't one of them. Most of us stayed inside the fence, so I didn't understand what it was like out here until I was on the ship."

14

"We can't just leave them here," Mellow said to Lena as they checked their own supplies for what they could spare. She couldn't just leave them to die from lack of food. Mellow had simply voiced her own thoughts. She needed to get tougher, but time for that later. These were really just kids.

"They're slowing us down," Lena said, unwilling to let Mellow know she was softening. "We can't keep helping them. Trish said they were going to deal with Trixie. I didn't ask for details."

"A day. We can spare that. It will give us a chance to help them find supplies. We'll be there if the traders come. They don't know how to fight, let alone survive to fight people like Trixie who are behind strong walls."

"They have a plant in the group," Lena said. "The longer we stay with them, the more likely we'll get caught up in whatever that person is doing."

"Or, we can watch and identify that person. Or, they aren't doing anything now they're free. What's wrong with you? Usually you want to help."

Mellow wasn't going to let it go. Lena thought about what would happen if she learned they'd been slaughtered. Something that could be avoided if they knew how to fight. Or learned how to hide. Or know who was betraying them. Was she doing the same as Trixie? Looking after her own people at the expense of others. Was that a good basis for any form of unity?

"I'm tired, I guess. Okay, we need to talk to the others without strangers around. Figure out where we're going. Then we'll know the best place to split off. I'm not letting them know where we are headed other than east."

In the end they agreed to stay together until Seattle. It would give Lena's team time to teach the kids some of the skills they needed, and possibly figure out who the traitor was. And it wouldn't drag anyone too close to Portland.

"Two days," Lena said to Trish and Ilsa. The two women had stepped into leadership roles. "Our priority is to get you weapons and survival supplies. Choose three people for weapons training."

Two days of sharing supplies and moving slowly. There was always a downside. Finding supplies for eight people would be much easier for them after they parted than it would be for this larger group.

THE FIRST DAY was easier walking than expected. It was cold, but it didn't rain or snow. They found winter coats for the kids in a camping store, but the rest of the store was stripped of the merchandise, taken or destroyed.

"That's petty," Ilsa said. "Why not leave it for someone else?"

"You'll see the same everywhere," Astrid said. "I haven't got an answer to why, but does it matter?"

"I guess not," Ilsa said. "We'll just have to make it to Pearl Two and take supplies from there when we move on."

"We need to get going," Scott called from the front door. "Everyone back here now."

Lena stood back and counted people as they arrived. Leaving anyone behind by mistake wasn't an option. Trish showed up last with the two youngest children in tow. They looked to be around ten or twelve and just as curious about the world as a pre-plague kid.

"They were digging into the bottom of the garbage bins," Trish said. "Good little scavengers."

The young girl looked at Trish with a frown. "We found some maps."

"Good," Scott said. "They'll come in handy for you. Keep them dry."

"Before we head out," Beattie said, stepping forward, "I found things you missed. Things you can use as weapons." She held out broken slats from a pallet, long shards of glass she'd wrapped in cloth. "Use your imagination next time."

15

They stopped for the night in a Costco. Someone had set fire to the tire supply outside, probably hoping to smoke out the person inside who'd locked the doors. But it hadn't worked.

"Something to be said for solid walls," Tik said. "Let me see the locks."

It took ten minutes to pick the lock and slide the door up. Whoever was inside had barricaded the entrance, making it impossible to enter without making a lot of noise shoving furniture away.

"Let one of the kids go," Astrid said. "They'll be able to squeeze in where we can't. Just to see if anyone is watching the door, not to go all the way in."

"That sounds like we're sending them to be killed," Beattie said. "You forgot to say we've been talking them through this all day."

"Look, we've made enough noise to draw someone out," Tik said. "The kid can slide through that gap and take a peek. No one else is small enough."

They were arguing with Lena when she hadn't said anything. *Am I that predictable?*

"It's a good idea," she said. "But it's not our decision. Trish or Ilsa should make the call."

"Bobby, do you think you can do it?" Ilsa asked one of the kids who'd kept exploring the camping store before.

"Sure."

He didn't wait for permission. Bobby shucked his jacket and wiggled behind an upended couch.

Lena was holding her breath. Despite her words, she couldn't help worrying. Back on the farm, Jason or Maya would have done the same thing at his age, but they had more experience than Bobby.

"There's a dead guy sitting in a chair," Bobby said. "It doesn't smell like anyone else is living there." He gave the couch a push. "He didn't build this deep."

Trish leaned against the wall as they waited for the barrier to open. Four of the strongest captives worked at it carefully, ensuring none of the components collapsed as they created an entrance.

"Get in," Beattie said. "We'll close this up and the doors to make it look like it's still locked up tight."

Ilsa led the group in, Trish staying to enter last. A good way to make sure no one wandered away.

The store was still packed with merchandise. They searched, but the dead man out front was the only inhabitant. He must have thought he was good for a long life inside and had been there enough time to get rid of the frozen food and perishables before they made the warehouse unlivable. The line of generators and propane tanks were evidence he'd had power to keep a chest freezer and microwaves running. Tik flicked a switch on one generator, but it didn't produce any power.

"Do we want to search for more fuel?" he asked. "Be nice to have a hot meal."

Ilsa shook her head and pointed over to where Siren and Trish were setting up a camp stove with Sterno. "We should get used to what we'll have. And nuked food isn't all that great."

Astrid was walking the center aisle, staring down each side before moving on. The others waited until she gave the all-clear and then they ran to grab whatever they could.

"Ilsa, you need to make sure they don't go overboard," Scott said. "They only take what they can carry. I don't know where they'll get horses."

"Yeah, but we can eat tonight. You can stock up. There's tons of stuff here for camping, clothes, equipment. Guns, ammunition. Other weapons. Bikes for transport and those buggy things that attach. We can take what we need to get to Pearl Two."

"Those guns aren't from their stock," Tik said. "That guy must have brought them in. Be careful, we don't know if they're in good condition."

In an hour, piles of supplies surrounded them. The dinner came from canned goods heated over the camp stove. Lena's team already had their loot stowed away, ready to take off in the morning. Trish and Ilsa had everything they needed to survive, and no amount of teaching over the next day would be worth hanging around.

"We'll set up a watch," Beattie said to Lena. "Just us. If there's a traitor in that group, we can't trust them."

Lena took the first watch. She slipped through the door and set up across the parking lot. The abandoned vehicles gave her good cover. She could see the entrance and turn to watch the road without much effort.

It was hard to believe no one had come back to fight

their way in for the treasure. The local people would have known what was inside. This or a Walmart would have meant the difference between dying and surviving early on.

The night was clear, and that meant icy. She pulled the sleeping bag around her and settled in. The burn marks from the tire blaze blackened the side wall of the building. She ran her gaze along the edge of the soot. It had almost reached the door. Perhaps the fumes had killed that man.

Something caught her eye. Beside the door, drawn in soot, was an arrow. Pointing upwards. Perhaps a sign that it was too dangerous to enter. Like the old hobo signs indicating safe harbor, or danger.

Maybe when they left, Lena would remove the mark. This goldmine should be open to all. Even the people who left behind destruction after taking what they needed or wanted. Supplies were too scarce now to deny anyone for the sake of just hoarding.

On second thought, maybe not. This wasn't her responsibility. It was hard enough to know who to trust and who to avoid. It might not be possible to join the country together right now, but it was vital they keep the farm safe. Leaving behind any evidence of their passing was too big a risk. Too many people already knew the general direction of the farm.

An hour later, she saw a shadow slip out of the building. Too soon for her relief. And there was no reason for anyone to leave. Only Lena's team knew there was a watch set up.

She watched as the shadow slipped around the building to the back. Then, checking to make sure the road was still clear, she left her hiding spot and crept along to follow.

Behind the building, someone had tried to bust through the loading bays. Their search inside showed the inhabitant had blocked these as well, using a heavy chain and padlock on the inside. It meant the only way dangerous people could enter was the front. Smart. If only he'd lived to see how effective his precautions were.

Lena stayed to the side of the building. It gave her a view of the loading area without having to step out and announce herself.

It was Trish. She had a can of spray paint and was marking the back of the building.

They are going east. It is day three. I will try to hold them.

16

L ena didn't move. Of all the people in that group of captives, Trish as the spy was the most surprising. But now Lena had witnessed her leaving the message, it made sense that she would step into the role. Leading gave her control, and access. The message would be covered over before either party left. But tonight was their last time together no matter how guilty she felt. Sometimes just taking care of your own was the right thing to do.

She slipped back to her hiding place. The road still needed to be watched. When Tik came to take the second watch, Trish would still be the spy, and she would think no one knew.

Tik moved silently toward Lena. She watched him slip from shadow to shadow with pride. Stealth was sometimes their only weapon, and he used it differently. They all did, in some ways. Astrid and Beattie hunted by creeping around in the darkness; Mellow, Scott, and Lena herself, used it to avoid notice; Luis just seemed to blend when he wanted to; Tik, he moved like an assassin, or maybe a cat burglar. He didn't have the ruthlessness of a professional killer.

As he neared, she reached out through the car window and snapped her fingers once.

He joined her. "Things are quiet inside," he said. "Scott added the new supplies to Angel. We'll have to take some bags too, but it means we can move fast without scavenging everywhere. Put a lot of distance between us."

Lena told him what she'd witnessed. "I'm going to tell them when I go inside."

"We'll go at first light no matter what," he said. "I thought she cared about those kids."

"Is it harder to believe because we trusted her? I mean, are we stupid, or just good people?" Lena asked. She'd continually struggled to stay on the good people side, but every instinct told her to protect her own and damn the rest.

"Good people," he said. "That doesn't mean we have to save everyone."

"Okay. The road is clear. I don't know if Trish expected the traders to come from the back, or knew they'd look for a message." That arrow made more sense to her now, a pointer to the message if her partners came from the front.

She would erase it before she slipped back in.

INSIDE, Scott waited for her with a can of chili warming on the stove. "Eat before we go. No point in leaving here hungry."

She wiped the soot off her fingers and took the spoon he held out. The food was nothing special, but it warmed her from her shift outside. "I need to talk to Siren," she said. He would tell her if Ilsa was suspect, too. Or who else could be trusted.

Siren approached her wrapped in a plaid couch throw. "I hope this is important."

"Brat." She gave him a playful punch. "It is. Your traitor is still at it."

"You know who?" He pulled the throw tighter around himself, as if it would protect him from the bad news.

"Who should I tell in that group?"

"Ilsa. She can be trusted."

"It's Trish," Lena said. "Are you sure Ilsa's not in on it?"

"Yes. How do you know it's her? For sure. You can't tell them if it's a guess."

"Lena wouldn't do that," Scott said. "Who is safe to talk to? Is Ilsa someone who can decide what they'll do?"

"Maybe Trish only did it on the ship. To survive?"

"She left a message for them tonight," Lena said. "I know it's hard to believe, but there is no doubt. She told them where we are going, or where we said, anyway."

"Ilsa," Siren said. "Just her. She'll figure out what to do."

Lena nodded to Scott, who left them to find Ilsa. "Do you want to stay around?"

Siren shook his head. "I'm not one of them. I'm still with you. Are we leaving now?"

"In the morning. We'll make it look like we're headed east, but we can't stay that way, at least at the beginning."

"I'll go back to sleep. I'll need the rest. I haven't been on horseback for a long time."

Lena remembered the aches of the first days tracking the ship. "It will be awful, but you'll recover fast."

Ilsa listened to the facts Lena laid out, her expression hardening as she heard the story. "I need to see the message," she said.

"Grab some spray paint. Don't let her see you." Lena looked to where the captives were spread out, sleeping. "Where is she?"

"Over in the corner," Ilsa said. "Can you get someone to tie her up without making noise?"

"I'll do it," Scott said. "And I'll get Astrid to guard her."

Ilsa rejoined Lena with a duffel bag full of black spray paint. "I have a couple of cans of yellow in there too."

Lena took her to the loading bay.

Ilsa read the words. "Bitch. Thank you for finding her." She put the duffel on the floor. "We'll cover it now and leave our own message."

It took only a few minutes to hide the words. The spray paint dried fast and Ilsa took two cans of neon yellow paint out. "You think I can spray again?"

"The new message will help hide the faint traces," Lena said. "Go ahead. It's not art, so a few blurs and streaks won't matter."

Ilsa shook the cans and then walked up to the wall. *We found her. Leave us alone or you'll join her in hell.*

"What are you going to do to Trish?" Lena didn't want to interfere, but the message made a promise that she didn't think Ilsa could manage.

"We'll decide when you're gone. It won't be pretty, but we should all agree."

17

The route turned east just as they saw the towers of Seattle. If they took the off ramp, the city would fade into the background. Lena felt the skin on her shoulders prickle. If the city wasn't as abandoned as they assumed, they could be turning their backs on a threat.

"Let's get a bit closer," she said. "Take a look from a high point."

"I'd like to know if it's been abandoned," Beattie said.

"We can go in for a quick look," Astrid said.

"I don't think that's a good idea," Lena said. "We need to know what's behind us when we head away from the coast. But I'm not ready for another surprise like Pearl Two."

Like Tik on the way out, she wanted to get off the highway. She was disturbed by the emptiness, something they hadn't encountered even in the desert areas on their way to the coast. Empty, and yet it still felt like someone was watching them. "They had a zoo. Maybe the predators escaped."

"Okay," Scott said. "The idea of a large cat stalking us is enough for me. But not all of us."

"I need to see," Lena said.

"Anyone else?" Beattie asked. When no one answered, she added, "I'll take Lena. You all wait here. We won't be gone long."

Lena nudged Bebop to follow Beattie to the side of an off ramp they'd passed a few minutes before stopping.

"There's no better vantage point unless you want to keep going on the I5," Beattie said.

Lena pulled her binoculars out of her pack and glanced around for a good observation point. "Just a few more feet along," she said. "We can see down one of the streets."

"There's a major intersection over there," Beattie said. "No more than a few feet. We're still hidden, but too close and we'll expose ourselves."

Lena scanned the street with the binoculars. There was no evidence of occupation. At least by humans. A pack of coyotes trotted across an intersection. A monkey sat on a fire escape. Only the monkey paid attention to them.

"I guess we know," Lena said. "Let's go back."

"You think Ilsa will be successful?" Mellow asked later as they traveled between two farms left to return to nature. "It feels a little cowardly to leave them to fight alone."

"I don't know," Lena said. "If it only takes sheer will, then yes. But they are young and inexperienced. I hope so. But that gang must be huge. I don't think it will last forever."

She didn't want to dwell on how they would replace Trixie and the others like her. How they would know who to trust. Everything she'd seen so far showed changing the person in charge wouldn't be a move for the better. Maybe clinging to the old ways was the problem. The towns around home were looking to the future and using what was available to thrive, not to hold onto the old world. Beta was the same, and a good part of Fort Revelation's success came from their isolation. Greenly could have easily taken over a vast part of the forest, but he kept to what they could manage.

Maybe her dream of a future couldn't work until enough communities gave up the past. If that was true, Lena wouldn't be the one driving change. She'd be old or dead by the time the world was ready.

"We'll be on the side roads by this afternoon," Tik said. "Camping tonight under the trees again. I never thought I'd look forward to sleeping outside."

"I need to go to Nicolette soon," Siren said. "We're headed in that direction. We could sidetrack."

"No." Lena was not going to let that woman drug them again. "We'll figure it out when we get close."

"But you need to go north to get back to your home," he said. The whine had crept back over the last day. "It wouldn't take much time."

"If you need to go back so badly, Beattie and I can take you," Astrid said.

"Let's talk about it later," Beattie said. "We need to fall into line now. The road is narrow and we're heading off soon."

Later, when they could look at a map, was a good idea, Lena thought. It was hard to judge how close they were when, even on horseback, travel was slow. This terrain was gentler than the mountains, meaning they would make good time, but roads didn't go in a straight line, none leading them to the farm anyway. That was a benefit when they were under the same roof.

They would need to veer north before finding a path south. And they hadn't really created a longer-term plan.

Just getting away from the gang and the captives without giving away their route had been enough.

"We can stop here for lunch," Luis called back a couple of hours later. "This is new territory for me, and I'd like to check where the next few places are."

Luis's choice turned out to be a rest area. One without a building, but the picnic tables were solid and there was a good place to leave the horses to feed on the grass.

"I'll scout," Astrid said. "We don't want surprises."

She ran off, leaving the rest to set up.

'I don't want to get into the habit of stopping for long breaks," Lena said. "But it is nice to get out of the saddle for a while. It's like I've never ridden before."

Astrid declared the site safe, telling them the building had been burned out a long time ago. Destruction of the toilet block but not the picnic benches wasn't that odd. Sometimes the rage that sparked the violence burned out fast. And nature still had the capacity to set fire to a building with a lightning bolt.

THEY ATE canned stew and corn heated over the camp stove; using the heaviest supplies first seemed like a good idea. If they ran out of fuel for the stove, the cans would be dead weight. Not every place they stopped was suitable for a fire. There was no guarantee they'd find communities who'd trade for a couple of tins of chili on their path.

"The farm is going to love the spices we brought," Mellow said, "until they run out. Think of what a real stew will taste like."

"Too bad there aren't any locked up mega stores left in our neighborhood." Scott took the dirty bowls to the stream.

"So, let's see where we are," Beattie said, nodding to the maps rolled up on the pile of supplies.

A faint sound of jingling reached them before anyone could make a suggestion. It grew closer, coming from the direction of the road.

"I'll go see," Beattie said. "Astrid, you wait here. It makes no sense for both of us to leave."

Lena gestured for everyone to clear away everything that would indicate they had something to steal. "If they're announcing their presence, they aren't likely trying to steal from us. But better to be safe."

"Or they're putting us off our guard," Astrid said. "You should go to the horses, Tik. Take Scott."

Beattie returned leading six monks. All dressed in brown robes, even in this cold without jackets. The sound was coming from tiny bells sewn into their sleeves. Rosaries hung from fingers that twisted the beads around. The only surprise was the sturdy hiking boots. Lena had expected rough sandals.

"These are the Brothers of Penance," Beattie said. "No weapons, no horses, no supplies I can find."

"We are nourished by God for our work," the tallest monk said. He topped out at about six feet three. "I am Brother Ambrose. These are my companions. Will you hear the word of our gospel?"

Lena had no use for their religion. People could believe whatever they wanted as long as they didn't force others, in her opinion. She wanted to say no but recognized the glint of determination in his eye. It would be faster to let them speak and then turn down their offer. Planning would have to wait until they were alone. "We can spare an hour," she said. "Do you have others in your...?"

"We are a monastic group," Ambrose said.

"Lena, we should go," Siren said. "We need to get more distance before nightfall."

"A little time is all we ask," Ambrose said. "We will rest here if you are leaving."

Lena pointed to the bench across from her. "I can't offer you anything, but we will listen."

The horses were sheltered under the trees. Ambrose and his brothers wouldn't know there were more than Beattie, Siren, and Lena. Astrid had slipped away as soon as it was evident that the visitors were coming, taking Luis with her. Lena hadn't noticed when Mellow left, but she was happy to present a weaker front. Perhaps the monks would decide they were too small a group to bother with.

Ambrose sat and indicated the others to find a place. They chose the closest two picnic tables, flanking Lena's position. Beattie and Siren stood back. The monks might have not intended to pose a threat, but their choice of seats was strategic.

"This is a good place to camp," Lena said. "Water, cover from the wind, and out of sight of the road."

"We often choose these places," Ambrose said. "In the past, they were rest stations. Now we like to think of them as places to restore one's soul."

18

"We have several miles to travel before we stop to camp," Lena said. "Please, let's hear what you want to tell us."

"It is the story of our world's salvation," Ambrose said. "God sent the plagues to remind us that we had strayed. That too many people were walking away from his path."

"Is your religion the only real one?" Siren asked.

His antagonistic tone was a good contrast to Lena's fake curiosity and Beattie's silence.

"A belief in God is a belief no matter the name assigned. I personally believe that when enough people return to religion, of any kind, God will reveal the one true path. We are gathering believers."

"Only men?" Beattie asked. "Does your brotherhood include women?"

"All are welcome, only some go out to harvest," Ambrose said in that tone Lena remembered from church. Pious, unwilling or unable to explain in detail, and a disdain for questions.

The choice of the word 'harvest' was troublesome.

"Is this what you wanted to tell us?" Lena asked.

"We share our beliefs. We explain the rites. We give directions to the safety of our church and home city."

"So, there's a city where all the believers live?" Lena couldn't imagine going back into a city any time soon.

"Not all," Ambrose said. "Others like us roam the country looking for people who wish to believe. Others farm and manage livestock. It is a wide community. And safe."

The other monks intoned something about the almighty keeping believers safe. And the jingling got louder as they shook their sleeves three times.

"Thanks, but we're not interested," Beattie said. "Right, Lena?"

"We will explain the rite of inclusion," Ambrose said. "Perhaps that will change your mind."

Saying no outright would keep him talking to convince them. He wasn't going to walk away without a solid attempt at converting them or being convinced they wouldn't bite. Lena wouldn't hold anyone back, but she also couldn't imagine any of her companions joining Ambrose. "If we still want to continue as we are after hearing about this rite, will you try to stop us leaving?"

"If that is what you truly wish," Ambrose said. "I will hear it from each of you and accept your answer." He looked into the distance behind Lena. "Young woman, please come closer so you might hear our words."

Lena thought Siren was the least likely to join up. He was in Nicolette's cult. She would make his decision. She wasn't here, but she would not agree anyway. And possibly Siren would be punished for even asking. She patted the bench beside her as Mellow appeared. "Come sit next to me," she called over her shoulder.

"And the warriors?" Ambrose asked. "Will they sit and join us?"

"We can hear fine," Beattie said.

By the time Ambrose took a breath in his droning about God's disappointment in humans and his grace in giving them a second chance, the sun was dipping. Lena had tried several times to get him to stop, but he was persistent.

"Thank you for the information," Lena said into the silence. "We need to move on."

"If you hold your journey for one more day, we can continue," Ambrose said as if he'd made progress.

"That is not possible," Lena said. "I will talk to my companions as we travel. If anyone wishes to join, they know where you'll be." She stood and walked away, ignoring his final words.

They gathered the horses and rode away from the rest area, out of sight of Ambrose so he had no chance to notice how big their group was. Or to insist on starting all over again.

"We're being watched," Astrid said.

"I figured that might happen. We'll get off the road as soon as we are sure they didn't follow. They'll know east, but not that we're headed a little north."

"So we're going to visit Nicolette?" Siren asked.

"I don't think that's a good idea," Lena said. "I want to learn more, not just see the same people on the way back." And I don't trust her, she thought.

"The path will fork soon," Beattie said. "Astrid and I will escort him. I also need to report."

"What will Astrid do after?" Siren asked. "That Greenly guy said no one could stay permanently."

"We'll convince him," Astrid said. "I'm not a kid anymore. I can contribute."

Beattie looked at Lena and smiled as if they shared a joke about Astrid's maturity. The girl had matured during her stint on Trixie's guard patrols. She still showed her kid side, but when it came to fighting or protecting the group, she became focused. It was difficult to remember that she was only seventeen sometimes.

"If he won't take her on, I'll stick with her. I'm sure Ilsa will be happy to have two fighters join up." Beattie nudged her horse forward to take the lead from Luis.

"He will," Astrid said. "She's just being cautious."

Lena left it alone. When they split off, she would miss all three, something she wouldn't have believed six months ago. "We'll check the map tonight," she said. "Figure out the best place for you to head north and our direction afterwards."

North had only been on her mind because the farm was in that direction. The strength of her need to return home surprised her. It seemed like her dream faded in the face of so much greed and inhumanity that her desire to be on the road waned, too.

There was still a lot of country between her and the farm. Just because the people they'd met on the trip out were less than excited about healing the land didn't mean everyone was. That gang couldn't be operating too far south. The distances were too much for them to be able to transport unwilling captives without damaging them. Doing it on land, where every stop was an opportunity for escape, was very different from at sea, on a ship.

Tonight, she would ask the others what they wanted to do before telling them her preferences. A different perspective might help. And tonight might be the last time there would be more than just the four who started, and Luis. Would he take the opportunity to move on when Siren, Astrid, and Beattie did? Lena hoped not. He might not always know the danger, but he had a familiarity with the country they needed.

19

Two days later, Beattie and Astrid led Siren north at a fork in the path. It hurt to see them go. As difficult as it had been to accept Astrid and Siren into the group, they'd both become family. Beattie had won Lena's heart the moment she partnered with Astrid and taught her how to be a warrior. Astrid had been affected, too. She'd pressed three of her precious knives in Lena's hand before launching herself on Raven's back.

"You might need them more than me," she'd said. "Maybe one day I'll come visit your farm and you can give them back."

Now, they stood beside their horses, looking out over a parking lot with only three cars from a vantage point on the approach road. No sign of the chaos from a final pillage of the stores. It was more disturbing than if the doors had been torn off and the ground littered with discarded items.

The feeling of abandonment that settled over every community they'd passed so far was amplified here. While the name of the town was a bit ominous, it was the penitentiary in Kansas that carried the weight in Lena's mind. What would the area around a place like the prison be like now? How many would have died in any of the huge federal prisons? Crowding, poor conditions, indifference; it would be millions.

This Leavenworth had been a cute little fake alpine village. Perhaps the memory of all the tourists who'd visited made the emptiness worse.

"Maybe all the survivors from the coast headed here," Tik said. "Good land for farming coming in the next few days. Easier to survive inland. They could be nearby."

"Because the gang forced them to move?" Mellow asked. "I can't see so many people deciding to migrate east without a major threat."

"Or they got into Pearl Two," Lena said. "Or Seattle has a community, despite what we saw. Or a combination of all those things. Setting up a farm is harder than just moving into one. And most of the fishing on the coast needs a boat."

"Does it matter?" Scott asked.

"It would be nice to know. If it's a new plague or some kind of raiders, we could be on the lookout at the farm." Lena nudged Bebop to a fast walk. "Let's get moving. Maybe what we find in Leavenworth will give us a better idea of the possibilities."

Someone had spray painted over the sign at the entrance to the Safeway.

This is a closed community. We are not interested. Do not go into the hills unless you are a fucking survivalist. We stay here. They stay there.

"Nice," Lena said. "You want to risk camping here, in the parking lot? Or do we move on?"

"Luis?" Scott asked.

"I never came this way. Figured it was all survivalist and bible thumpers. It's worth a look. No scavenging."

"And we set a watch," Tik said. "If they leave us alone, fine. If they come, we leave."

The light was fading, and Lena smelled snow in the air. "I think we should move on," she said. "We're not desperate yet. I don't fancy running away in the middle of the night if it starts to rain, or worse."

"The hills they mentioned on the sign are likely behind us," Luis said. "I think a quick look around is a good idea either way."

"I'll go," Tik said. "You check the map, see how far the next town is." He dismounted and skulked across the parking lot.

"We stay visible," Luis said. "Look like we're passing through."

Lena wound one of the flashlights while Scott and Luis opened the map on the ground. Mellow placed small rocks around the edges to hold it.

"Head toward Wenatchee? There are five places between us and there," Lena said, pointing to the path. "Probably a few rest stops on the way for a camp."

"We can only go a few more hours," Scott said. "I don't want to lose the horses to injury."

"We can maybe get to Dryden," Luis said, "with time to do some reconnoitering."

"That's your best bet." The voice made all of them jump.

A man stood ten feet away. Tall, bulky, and holding a rifle. Lena didn't trust anyone who relied on guns these days. Either it was just for show, or the previous owner was killed. Even refilling the rounds would be dangerous after all this time.

"We're just passing through," Scott said. "No need for any problems."

"Why did your man go into the store?"

Lena indicated the others should stow the map. "I'm Lena. What's your name?"

"No need for pleasantries," he said. "Answer the question."

"We've been on the road long enough to know it's smart to see what's at your back," she said. "You heard us, right? We aren't planning to stay."

"Why haven't you found a place to hunker down? Plagues died out years ago. Not many people still walking."

"We have a home," she said. "We're exploring. Trying to find out what's happening in the world."

"Nothing," he said and then spat to the side. "People surviving. People taking what they need. Am I wrong?"

Lena almost let the argument slip out. He wasn't looking for a debate, and they were lucky he'd decided to talk rather than attack. "Sure. You know anything about south?"

"Heard some rumors. Fools trying to remake the world. You keep going on that road, you'll find them." He tilted his chin toward the east. "You'll see some signs when you get closer."

He meant it as a warning, but Lena hoped he was wrong about the 'fools' part. Maybe it was finally a place they could talk to about unity. Her dream for alliances was feeling more out of touch with reality every day. It would be nice to get a little hope. "We'll be on our way as soon as he gets back."

"He's coming. You still here by the time I get back from my patrol, and you'll regret it."

The man faded into the shadows.

"Looks like everything is gone. From the Safeway, and the little stores."

"We're leaving," Luis said.

20

It started snowing an hour after they left Leavenworth. Riding in the dark was bad enough, but the wet and cold seemed to drain any hope from Lena's soul. They had no chance of reaching Dryden. Now, they were scanning for the closest shelter with a roof. In a few more miles, Lena thought she'd probably settle for a tarp and a damp spot under the trees so they could huddle together against the chill.

"We should take the next turn off," Scott said. "There's likely to be a gas station, or some kind of store. We'll have the horses inside tonight."

Lena looked up from Bebop's neck. It was the least uncomfortable position that would protect her from the driving snow. "Okay. We need to keep focused on where we're going, though. Not get sidetracked just because we took shelter."

He nudged Beauty forward to join the others.

The off ramp turned out to be a good decision when they found it. Two gas stations, a cafe and a tourist store.

The dust and vermin droppings inside every building were evidence that no one had been near the area for years.

Lena didn't care for the ease of access. Beattie would have told them to keep moving, she was sure. The roads were in fairly good shape and gave access to anyone traveling from all directions. There was no sign that people or horses had been through since the snow started. The upside was they'd see someone coming. At least when it was light. They chose the gas station on the south side where the cafe and tourist trap gave them more room.

They put the horses in the tourist shop. It was the largest space, and moving the shelves of postcards, teeshirts, and key chains gave the animals room to walk around a little. Another place no one had bothered to loot.

"Who's going to stay with them?" Tik asked.

"Should we all?" Mellow asked. "There's room, and we don't smell that great either. We can clean away the worst of the debris."

Lena glanced into the corners, checking for signs they weren't the only creatures looking for a dry camp. Everything looked old, and the smell of the vermin was dry rather than fresh. "Why would the rats leave?"

"I don't think there's food left," Tik said. "They'll have gone looking for a better place to nest."

The anxious feeling in her gut that this all looked too good to be safe wasn't satisfied with his answer. But it made sense. And they would all sit guard shifts. "I guess we've stayed in worse places."

"Not much," Scott said. "Be careful sweeping a clean space. Breathing in the dust from vermin poop can give us diseases."

"There are clear spaces," Lena said. "We'll just take those and leave the mess in place."

"So, when the next person comes along, they'll only know someone was here by the piles of horse dung?" Luis asked. "It's better than risking death by Hantavirus."

In the end, they pulled out tarps to cover an area large enough for them to sleep close to each other. The tarp could be cleaned easily, and sleeping bags couldn't.

"I'll take first watch," Tik said. "We'll do short shifts, so no one falls asleep on duty."

They were all exhausted by the events of the day. First, encountering the man who could easily have shot them all — lack of ammunition was more likely the reason than some human empathy. The weather, the darkness and, to be honest, the eeriness of the empty buildings. Lena's thoughts spiraled downward. She needed to do something.

"Two hours," Lena said. "Not a second longer. And we leave as soon as we see light."

"Dinner outside?" Mellow asked. "I guess I can manage to sleep here, but I don't want to eat in a rat's toilet."

The gas station canopy was still in one piece, so it gave them cover. No one wanted to risk a fire near an unknown quantity of gasoline and diesel, so it was dried meat and fruit washed down with water.

"It's late March, right?" Tik asked.

Lena estimated the time it took them to rescue the captives. They'd left Pearl Two a week earlier than planned, so about the middle of February. "I guess it could be just about April, but maybe still March?" she said. "Why? We don't usually worry too much about dates."

"This could be the last of the bad weather," Tik said. "On the farm, they'll be planting in a couple of weeks. This is farther south, so maybe no more snow?"

"Luis? What do you think?" Lena wanted them to go to

sleep with a positive in their minds. Even one as shaky as the weather.

"Could be," he said as if he sensed her feeling. "Weather is still kind of unpredictable, but I don't remember late snows, at least anything that stuck around."

"We should go back in," Tik said. "The gas station toilet is still flushing if you want to take care of anything. It must be working from a tank on the roof. Sink water isn't, so you'll need to wash your hands with drinking water."

Lena made a note to label some of the empty bottles as non-potable, so they didn't waste clean water. She was too tired to do it now, or to mention it. "I'll take the second watch," she said.

They were settled inside. Tik sat on an overturned crate at the door with his bow and a knife beside him. The others were in sleeping bags close together on the tarp. The horses were quiet except for the occasional nicker. If she closed her eyes and didn't breathe too deeply, everything was peaceful.

She curled into Scott's back and emptied her mind. Tik would wake her soon enough. No point in staying alert.

Her mind had a different plan. The minute she tried to relax into sleep, her head filled with worries about uncompleted tasks and ideas — most of which were only in her head. She tried not to deal with regret, but tonight all she could do was question her stupid decision to leave the farm. If they got back, she was never doing that again.

"Someone's coming," Tik whispered. "More than one someone."

Lena nudged the others awake, and in moments they were standing in the shadows armed and ready to defend the camp.

"Did you see who?" Scott asked.

"I've got the horses," Luis said. "Don't want them trampling us in a panic."

"There's five, maybe more behind them. On foot, no horses or bikes. I don't know if it's someone from Leavenworth or the hills around here. That notice said to stay away from the hills, and that might include here."

"We're ready," Lena said. "This place is defensible. No back door, and the only glass is the entrance."

"They might not look here," Mellow said. "It's a good rest place. They might not be trouble, just travelers like us."

They hadn't encountered any other groups in days. And even before that, only the occasional hunting party.

The front door moved, and a man stepped through. He was wearing a brown robe and carrying a sword.

21

Lena gripped her knife tighter. These monks weren't here to convert them. It was too much of a coincidence for her to believe Ambrose was innocent of this attack.

She hoped everyone remembered Beattie's lessons and held back until the enemy committed.

She felt Mellow beside her rebalance her weight, ready to defend against anything. The horses moved nervously in the back. A rear door would have come in handy to get them out of harm's way. She had to trust Luis would take care of them. She needed to focus on her job right now and not worry about the others. Everyone was capable of doing what was needed.

The monk entered, followed by another. They split up, each shifting to the side so they could cover more directions. When all five were inside, the first two started moving down the far aisles. It was dark, but the presence of the horses gave away any hope of a surprise defense. If Lena could see them, it wouldn't be long before the monks found her.

She nudged Scott and then pointed at the approaching men.

He nodded and silently directed Tik down the opposite aisle.

The monks outnumbered them, but not by much. Three were guarding the door, probably hoping to block escape or capture the horses. Or, to come in a second wave if the first one didn't take them all out.

Lena and Mellow focused on the three still at the entrance. Keeping quiet was the best tactic right now. Not that the fight could be avoided, but delay worked in their favor, not the attackers'.

A grunt came from her left, then a scrape on the floor. Someone was down.

Before she could worry that Scott had lost his fight, a shout came from her right.

Tik and the monk on that side were locked in a battle. Tik's knife aimed at the man's eye, the monk holding him off with both hands, his own weapon somewhere out of sight.

"Go," Lena said. "We'll take the two in front and hope Scott survived to take on the other one."

The two guards were distracted by the sounds of Tik's fighting and didn't notice Lena or Mellow until they screamed defiance and ran into them.

Lena's opponent managed to slice her arm before she shoved her knife into his throat. As he fell, she grabbed his sword and turned to the remaining monk. Shouting to be heard over the screams of the panicked horses, she pointed the blade at his chest and demanded answers. "How many more?"

"I won't tell you," he said.

He tried to raise his weapon, but Mellow kicked it out of his hand.

"Tell me," Lena said. "I'll let you live if I believe you."

Luis had calmed the horses now that there was no overt fighting, so no need to shout.

"How will you believe me?"

Scott moved up beside Lena. "I'll go look. If he tells you the truth, then I'll be able to confirm it."

He slipped around the monk and through the door, his own knife and bow in his hands.

There was a grunt from the direction of Tik's fight and then the thud of another body falling.

Lena knew better than to look. Any distraction gave her prisoner a chance to run.

"I'm okay," Tik called out. "Move him from the door so he can't escape. I'll help Scott."

"Wait." Lena used the sword to urge the man to the side. "Can we leave when we've finished with him?"

"Yes, but I can't leave the horses," Luis said. "We didn't unpack much, so it won't take long for us to go."

As much as she wanted Scott protected, leaving was more important. "Tik, either help me here or go pack up."

Tik stepped up beside her.

"I'll take care of it," Mellow said. "You know I don't like killing more than one attacker a day."

That tactic was all Astrid. Make the other guy think you're more dangerous than you are.

"If he comes back with information before you tell me, I have no reason to keep you alive."

The man glared defiance and pressed his lips together as if sealing off the possibility of talking.

"Fine. I don't have a problem killing an enemy," she said. "I was going to let you live, but you're right, that's way too risky."

He licked his lips and looked down at the blade. "You will kill me anyway."

"How many?" Tik asked.

"Why should I tell you?"

"That's more like it," Lena said. "What's the price for the information?"

"I live." He looked up from the blade. "I am not ready to go to God yet."

"Isn't that up to him?" Scott asked as he stepped back inside.

"I am still alive, so I think he has more use for me here."

That kind of faith is usually painted over some kind of hypocrisy, Lena thought. "How many?"

"None," he said. "Not here. Ambrose thought we could take care of you. He didn't want to take too many off the mission."

"And what happens when you don't report back?" Lena raised the weapon again to remind him that she was a threat.

"He's too far away to worry about," the monk said.

"What was the mission?" Scott asked. "The one you left."

"We are gathering followers for God."

"And killing people who don't believe?" Scott asked.

"Unbelievers will weaken our link to God. You had your chance."

"Okay, that's enough," Lena said. "Tie him up."

Tik reached for him while Scott held a knife to the man's throat.

"Why are you leaving me here to die?" he asked. "You said I would live."

"You'll figure out how to escape," Mellow said. "Just because we can kill doesn't mean we like it."

Lena watched as the man pulled away from Tik. "No. I cannot stay here. God is calling me to another path."

"One that has you sneaking up on us again?" Lena asked.

He went still. Tik reached for his arm again.

"God welcome me for my deeds." As the words left his lips, the man jolted forward, impaling himself on Scott's blade.

They all jumped back, but the blood gushed so fast it sprayed them.

22

There was no further trouble over the next few days. As they got past the old border with Idaho, signs appeared. Not many, and nothing that promised safety or acceptance, but pointing the way. The man in Leavenworth had told them they'd see the invitations. Glass House, which was the name of the town or community or whatever it was, stood close to McCall, Idaho. Another community of abandoned buildings and empty streets. They'd bypassed it after seeing the streets from the road. Someone had gone out with a blast, a building blown up and fire scorch still staining the roads.

"Maybe everyone went to this Glass House," Mellow said. "If there was a safe place, we would have gone, right? Instead of to the farm. That sign back at McCall said population was just under three thousand. The survivors could only be three to five hundred people."

Her logic worked for the resort town, but not for all the emptiness behind them. The monks couldn't be the only ones preying on the hopeless. The gang trafficking people, the survivalists in the hills. Normal death by accident or old age, or murder. Lena shivered at the last.

What they'd done wasn't murder. The thought didn't comfort her any more today than it had every day since.

"We need to set up somewhere to observe, first," she said. "I don't want a repeat of Pearl Two."

"The horses," Luis asked. "Do we keep them outside again?"

"Always," Tik said. "We can't give anyone a way to trap us."

"We'd leave the horses behind if we had to," Lena said, "but I agree. Leaving them safe somewhere is a good move. The bulk of our supplies, too."

"Should be a stable around here," Luis said. "We can leave them alone for a while. A week, if there's food and water available. It'll stink when we get back, but the horses won't care."

"Let's discuss that when we figure out what to do," Mellow said. "Unless you think we should split up? A couple of people look for a vantage point and the others find a place to leave the horses?"

"The days are still too short to do anything else." Lena motioned for them all to stop and cross to a clearing beside the road. "We need to find a place fast. This is a resort town. There's a lake. Probably a good place to find a stable. And we're about a mile from the turn off the signs mentioned."

"We can't split up," Tik said. "If Astrid and Beattie were still with us, it would be different. But we don't have enough people. We go to the lake and find a place to hole up and stable the horses. Tomorrow, someone stays there to set it up, and the others go looking for somewhere to spy on Glass House."

"We could stay here a couple of days," Lena said. "Think out our decisions before we act."

"Check for other predators," Luis said. "Wolves, bears, anything posing a danger to the horses. Some of them are getting hungry in this weather."

"We need to put a deadline on it," Lena said. "Three days? If we can't decide what to do, we keep going toward Boise."

"Okay," Scott said. "Let's find that place to hang out."

THE STABLE THEY found near the lake had rooms in the loft. Hay still sat in bales, no smell of mold or other problems. The horses would be fine for long enough to assess Glass House from the inside. And it was close enough to the settlement that someone could check on them every day if it made sense.

"I guess we need to figure out how to assess the risk from the outside," Lena said, "and we aren't staying long, even if it's safe."

"A week at most," Tik said. "The weather will be better every day now."

"An escape route," Luis said. "One entrance means we'll be trapped."

"If it's inside a building, we won't see anything," Mellow said. "Are we still willing to keep moving if we don't get enough information in three days? I don't know if we need to take a week."

Lena hated the idea of missing out on a large community. Especially after all the abandoned ones. If this Glass House place was thriving, regardless of the reason, they would learn what happened. The assumption it was a voluntary migration was unsupported by fact. What if this was the new threat? One that would eventually arrive at the farm doorstep.

"We only move on if we see something dangerous," she said. "If we can't decide, we split up. Maybe all of you stay here and just Scott and I go in."

"If something goes wrong, you won't be able to tell us," Tik said.

"We'll figure out some contingencies if it comes to that," Lena said. "Maybe when we see what kind of observation post we find."

"First light," Scott said. "The last one on watch can wake us, and we'll start looking for a spy nest."

LENA WAS THE FIRST WATCH, as usual. She found it hard to sleep after being woken during the night, so starting on alert gave her an unbroken time for rest. It didn't always mean sleep, but it was rest.

Luis took the last shift. He would stay behind and could rest while the others searched.

"We split into pairs," Tik said. "Reconnoiter until midday, and then come back to report."

"Is everyone's watch showing the same time?" Mellow asked.

Precise time didn't mean anything these days. When they checked, the watches were all within ten minutes either way.

"I think Mellow and I should go together," Lena said. "We know Glass House is south and a bit east of here. Scott, you and Tik should go over the hills to the east. Mellow and I will head south. We should be able to find something covering that range."

"We won't get far in a couple of hours," Tik said, "unless the viewpoint is just at the top of the hills."

"It tells us something, even if we don't find a clear view close by," Lena said. "If we can't see them, they won't be able to see us. We're fine here to spend a couple of days looking."

"I'll fish while you're gone," Luis said. "Saw some tackle downstairs."

23

Lena and Mellow reached the road and followed it for half the allotted time. They came to an intersection that should lead them closer to their destination. "There's no guarantee we'll find a place to observe," Mellow said. "In fact, this road is heading lower and might turn us to face the entrance."

"True. I don't want to be seen by whoever lives there before we have a plan of action." Lena nudged Bebop in a circle. "We can go back. Maybe the boys found something."

"There was that rest area," Mellow said. "Not an observation post, but maybe there's some kind of information board. There were at the other ones."

"Maybe a map," Lena said, "for tourists. Businesses would pay to be listed on there. And we've been focused on finding a high point. I think we should try to figure out what this place was before. Glass House is an unlikely name for a town."

Lena and Mellow returned to the camp to find Scott and Tik already there. Was that a good sign?

"Sit, I'll put the fish I caught on the fire," Luis said.

"Never been so easy to catch dinner. Like they forgot anything about hooks and lures being dangerous. We can all talk while we eat."

"There's a vista point," Scott said when he'd cleaned his plate. "We need to find a way to obscure the binoculars so we don't alert them with a flash from the lens. We'll see the traffic or movement inside a bit, but no details. It's too far away."

"It used to be a giant agribusiness," Lena said. "Big enough to be put on the map as a local site. Or big enough to pay to be put there."

THEIR VANTAGE POINT wasn't as helpful as Lena had hoped. Yes, they could see Glass House. People came and went during the day. No one seemed to be running away or being forced to enter. No sign of people being forced to work didn't mean they weren't. They spent two days taking turns watching.

Someone was maintaining the walls from when it was a business. Two entrance points faced the road. One through some kind of building, for people-sized visitors. The other was a sliding panel in the wall big enough for wagons.

Lena fought to keep her memories of the farm from coloring her observation. This was a much bigger enterprise, but it was still growing food.

On the third evening, Lena asked for a decision. "If we aren't going in, we need to move from here. I'm starting to feel too comfortable."

"We need to go in," Tik said. "All of us."

"If we pass up the opportunity, then we aren't really looking for allies," Mellow said. "If that's the case, we should head home."

Lena's doubts had followed her from Portland. Without being able to talk to other communities, all she had was Trixie's betrayal and deserted towns. "We need to know," she said. "My vote is to go in."

"I agree," Luis said. "This place wasn't putting out invitations when I last came through. I never heard of it. So, something happened around here. The horses will be fine. I'll come back after a couple of days if you want to stay longer. Just to check on them."

"It's going to take us a while to walk there," Scott said. "We can leave most of our stuff up here. It's basically hidden from below."

"We should leave here at first light," Mellow said. "Make sure it looks like we've been traveling, so some supplies in our packs."

The posters weren't exactly invitations, Lena thought. "There's a third option. I know we didn't want to get separated, but I did volunteer Scott and I to go there while you wait."

Luis fed a small branch to the fire. "I don't know if we should. Look, I know I've usually stayed outside, but that last stretch I spent most of the time worrying if something went wrong. It got better when you came to visit, but never went away. I stayed outside the cult without a problem, sure. I knew what was going on in there, and we hadn't been together very long."

"I'm not willing to wait here and worry," Mellow said.

Tik took her hand and squeezed. "Like I said, I think we all go. If something turns out to be bad, the more of us to fight our way out, the better. If it's good, then we all get to see for ourselves. Some of us could bring the horses and supplies in."

Lena couldn't argue the logic. If they split up and something went sideways, the ones inside Glass House would be forced to run back to the camp. Together, they could go anywhere. If it came to the worst, the horses could be abandoned. But it would have to be very bad for them to let that happen.

"Okay, tomorrow at first light. I guess the horses will be okay."

"Yeah, no sign of wolves or anything big enough to take a horse down," Luis said. "We'll lock them in just to be sure."

THEY MADE it to the gate of Glass House by mid-morning. Their backpacks contained a few days' worth of supplies and clothes. Sleeping bags rolled and attached to the sides. Lena hoped they looked like people who'd spent weeks on the road. Not like they'd left all their possessions back with the horses and were prime to rob.

The smaller entry was open, but the inside wasn't lit well enough to see in. The wagon gate was closed with a chain wrapped through the handle and padlocked. Either the people in charge were worried about raiders, or it was just normal protection.

"I don't see any guards," Tik said.

"There must be some inside," Lena said. "It wouldn't be prudent to just let people wander in. Let's just remember to stay alert and not get fooled."

"There was no way we would have seen what Trixie was up to," Scott said, "if we'd had a chance to look."

Lena had spent hours mulling that over, and she didn't agree. Maybe they hadn't had a chance to watch from outside, but Trixie's actions toward Siren were definitely about grooming him when looked at in hindsight. That alone should have told them to leave. The relief at being rescued made her blind to the red flags. This time, she wouldn't let that happen.

"Lead the way," Tik said to Luis. They'd agreed to let him seem the leader this time. His life of traveling made him the most likely to spot problems.

24

"Welcome to Glass House."

The words came from a boy who looked about ten years old. Behind him were three people well-armed and ready to protect him. The place got its name from the building they stood in. A small, traditional glass greenhouse. Nothing was planted here, and it was clearly being used as a lobby for the community.

What message are they sending? Lena watched the reactions as Luis explained who they were and that they were looking for a place to rest for a couple of days.

"I'm Sylvester." The boy pointed at the three protectors. "Don't worry about them, you seem like nice people."

There must be more to getting inside, Lena thought as she looked around. The three protectors didn't seem to be sending the boy signals. There was no one else in sight. She wanted to reach out to Luis and say they should go. But if asked, she wouldn't have been able to explain. It was possible that the boy was being indulged with this position and the real test would come when they walked through the back door into Glass House.

"Is there a price?" Luis asked. "We can pay with work, but we don't have much of value on us. There isn't really much of value but labor to trade these days."

"We'll see," Sylvester said. "Follow me. You have to fill out some paperwork, and then Marnie will decide if you get to be a guest or a worker."

He turned to the back door. The three armed protectors separated, one right behind the boy, the other two flanking their group. That explained why the room didn't have any plants. Space to maneuver was more valuable than a little more room to grow food, at least in here.

The next space was open to the weather. A table sat to the right with ten chairs and sheets of paper, each with a pencil. Walls of buildings formed the sides, and the back was the open door to what had been a warehouse. Sylvester told them to sit and wait for Marnie. Then, he and his escort returned to the tiny glass house.

The paper was turned face down but so thin that the three questions written in block letters showed through as shadows.

"I feel like I'm waiting to be sorted," Luis said. "I was clear we weren't interested in staying. I guess we answer honestly."

Honestly according to their cover story. Luis was talking for the benefit of whoever might be listening. "There's not much to say," she said. "We've been walking for months, not much has happened."

A woman came out of the warehouse. Hiking boots, plaid shirt, dirty blue jeans, hair held tightly back in a ponytail.

"I guess this might sound weird," she said. "Testing people who just want to stay for a day or two. But we lived this long being careful." She nodded toward the sheets of paper. "Here's how it works. You stay out here until we decide to let you in, or you decide to take off. You answer the questions. We work out if you're trouble. You meet with me and then the decision gets made. No one gets hurt. You don't pass inspection, you go on your way."

"I guess we should get started," Luis said. "Will you watch us? Like a proctor?"

"I'm not standing over you. Plenty of people inside watching. Been a while since we had so many travelers all at once. They get curious."

"Okay," Luis said. "Let's get this over with."

Lena turned over the paper and read the three questions.

What did you do before it all went to shit?

What's the worst thing you did to survive?

What skills have you learned?

The monks were pretty bad, Lena thought, but they'd already agreed not to mention the attack.

Lena wrote the answers truthfully.

Teacher. Killed defending my home. Everything you need.

25

The community didn't have a lot of rules. Marnie told them not to provoke a fight, don't expect people to talk about their past, and don't stay past the three days. There was no fee to stay, but to have access to more than just the basics, they took on work in the poly tunnel that produced leafy vegetables and tomatoes. It was one of fifty spread across the vast, open land.

The living quarters were in the old admin and processing buildings at the entrance, the rest of the property was set up to produce food, from lettuce to mushrooms. Each tunnel had been modified to work with solar power.

In the farthest reaches of the land were livestock, sheep, chickens, goats, and a few cows. There weren't enough people in the buildings to need this much food. Lena spent as much time as she could over their three days trying to find out where the excess was going. The only way in for a wagon was the front, unless she'd missed some back door. So, all of it must be local. But who were the locals? The land had been empty and abandoned the whole way.

In the morning, all five were sent to work in the poly tunnel with an existing team.

"It's pretty simple," the man assigned to them said. "In here, we're preparing for the season. You'll check on the seedlings and look for dry spots, rips in the cover, and pests."

"Is this happening in each tunnel?" Luis asked.

"Depends," the man said. "I'll let Sweeney answer your questions, he's been around a while, worked the different seasons. I'll get through my part and then you get to work."

Sweeney turned out to be a slight man who was working close by. He looked like he'd been a farmer all his life. The tough, sun-damaged skin, the strong hands. Before he came to Glass House, he worked outside.

Their instructor told them how to tell if a pest was beneficial or damaging and what to do with each. Then he left them to work.

"So, Sweeney," Scott said, "you've been here a while?"

"Worked the farm before," he said. "Didn't realize I'd be babysitting, but let's get you working. We have a quota."

We can work and talk, Lena thought. Staying here was about learning. If they just followed orders, how would she know if Glass House was a place to talk about her dream of unity?

"How do you get the beneficial bugs?" she asked.

"Had some before," Sweeney said, not looking up from the soil. "Kind of an 'if you build it' thing these days."

"What's in the other tunnels?" Mellow asked. "I can't imagine you need so much of the same produce."

"Don't talk about stuff outside my job," Sweeney said. "Other tunnels got root veg, tomatoes. One is hot enough for a few exotics, like bananas."

"Coffee?" Lena asked. If any place could grow beans, it would be here.

"Nope. Never got the starters. No chocolate either."

"Pity," Lena said. "Do you miss them?"

"Grateful for what Marnie created here," he said. "I do what I'm told for the sake of the community."

The rest of the day was spent bending over tiny seedlings and pulling out anything that didn't look completely healthy.

THE SECOND MORNING, Mellow had been called to work the infirmary. The others stayed in the tunnels. This time they were working with root vegetables. The protection the poly cover gave allowed Glass House to grow them almost all year. Lena wondered if they would be able to install some at the farm. Maybe start small.

Sweeney wasn't assigned to the same, so they worked with a woman called Eva.

"Have you been here a long time?" Lena asked as soon as the instructions were given.

"A year," she said. "Used to work in these things before. In the forest. Not exactly a legal crop."

"We were talking to Sweeney yesterday," Luis said. "Is he around?"

"He's doing whatever he's been told to do. We all work for the benefit of the community. You should get to work."

The tunnel was humid and warm, and everyone was dressed for the cold outside. It wasn't long before outer clothes were shucked and sitting in a pile at the entrance. Getting to stay together in the barracks and having a shower every day didn't seem like a fair exchange for the back-breaking work. It also cut into their time for gathering information. Mellow's reassignment should give them a deeper understanding of the whole community.

"How do I get to talk with Marnie?" Lena asked. What she'd observed led her to believe dropping by would be considered rude. Everything had a process and a list of requirements.

"You planning to apply for residency?" Eva asked. "Do this kind of thing until you can't?"

The idea that she'd work in the tunnels for the rest of her life didn't appeal to Lena. She didn't mind hard work, but everyone needed a change. "Do people live long if this is what they do every day?"

"Hard work never killed anyone," Eva said. "You want to talk to Marnie about staying, you better check your attitude."

Lena let the subject go. The more she heard from the people she met, the less she wanted to ask Marnie to join an alliance. Granted, she'd only encountered Eva and Sweeney, but both of them were curt and unfriendly. Nothing she could point to that made her certain something was awry, but definitely a bad feeling.

"Because no one says anything negative," Luis said when she brought it up later in their shift. "Not even after a few drinks. Everyone is satisfied with their life."

THAT EVENING, Luis convinced them to stay in the dining hall. "Won't learn anything unless you talk to people who've had a few drinks," he said. "Just be careful. There's a game in the back corner, no stakes, just for fun. I'll see what I can get going."

"He's right," Scott said. "People loosen up after work." He walked off to find a different group to join.

Lena sat where she was with Mellow and Tik. "I've never been good at mixing," she said. "Let's see if anyone comes to us."

"Good luck with that," Mellow said. "I see the other two nurses. I want to introduce Tik. They thought you were cute."

Suddenly alone, Lena tried not to look like she was spying while she observed. She looked around for Sweeney. Not because she thought he'd talk more about the community, but to make sure he was okay. His disappearance was just one more vague hint at trouble.

No sight of him. As much as she tried to anticipate hindsight wisdom, Lena couldn't grab onto anything.

Sylvester joined her just as she was thinking of leaving.

"Hi, you have one more day with us," he said. "Just wondering if that's changed."

"I think we'll leave tomorrow," she said. "Is that okay?"

"Leave when you want. I heard you wanted to talk to Marnie," he said. His tone told her that was the real reason he'd joined her.

"If she's available," Lena said.

"What about?"

"Personal matter," Lena said. "It's not important. I'm sure she's busy."

"She is," he said. "I'm sorry you decided to go. You all worked really hard, even though this isn't your community."

He left before she could thank him.

26

The others joined Lena in their corner of the barracks an hour later. "We should leave tomorrow," she said as they settled. "Unless you learned something tonight that says we should stay."

"Not much," Mellow said. "I did hear what happens with the excess produce."

"So, there is too much for this place," Scott said. "I was beginning to think there must be an army hidden somewhere. Just eating until someone sent them off to war."

"There are places farther south," she said. "Wagons go trading with the produce. Not like in Liberty. They kind of go to the customers. It's in exchange for things scavenged or services. Like the wool from the sheep and goats is processed a day's ride from here. And the sheets to repair the tunnels are brought in when they're found."

"There are a lot of young people here," Luis said, "doing jobs like Sylvester. Things usually done by adults."

"You think they're trading for kids?" Lena asked.

"I think they use people efficiently," he said. "The kids don't look abused or scared. Youngsters don't have the stamina to work on the land this many hours. And if they were into that kind of trade, some of the adults would be angry. I can't believe no one would notice. This place isn't like Pearl Two. No convenient gang activity outside to explain people disappearing."

"So it seems to be exactly what they told us," Mellow said. "People working together. No troublemakers. Working with their neighbors. Isn't that your vision, Lena?"

"Yeah," Lena said. "But why does it all seem creepy?"

"Because no one says anything negative," Luis said. "Not even after a few drinks. Everyone is satisfied with their life. It has to be an act."

Luis's words resonated with Lena's worries. "My dream isn't some kind of happy utopia. People aren't like that."

'It's not drugs," Mellow said, "or it's not drugs we're getting. There was nothing in the infirmary except basics. And we haven't changed or forgotten anything, right?"

"I didn't see Sweeney anywhere," Lena said. "He's the only one who seemed even slightly disgruntled. Remember he didn't like babysitting us?"

"Maybe he got reassigned?" Mellow said. "Like me? They needed someone to help in the infirmary, so I got sent there."

Lena hoped she was right. If Marnie only kept the people who were willing to do as she asked without complaining, then there must be a lot of culling. Perhaps that was why the kids worked the admin jobs. In fact, as she thought about it, it wasn't just kids. Every one of the guards looked similar. All about the same height, weight, and body type. The people she'd seen working the tunnels again fit a type. If they'd been able to explore the entire complex, would the livestock team all look like cowboys?

"So, are we leaving tomorrow?" she asked. "If there are

all these customers south of here, we can talk to them. It's not our job to fix things the way we want them."

Maybe the people south would know exactly what happens to anyone who has different ideas. The thought gave Lena chills.

"I'm ready to go. You notice every time you ask someone about living here, they say pretty much the same thing," Tik said.

"Like they're afraid of being caught out?" Mellow asked. "Now I regret working in the infirmary. I could have asked way more questions if I wasn't being watched all the time."

"What kind of injuries or illness?" Luis asked. "I didn't see any accidents, but they needed you right away."

Mellow closed her eyes and started listing off the patients. "A boy with a broken finger, I think he said he jammed it in a door that was closing. A woman with a bad burn from the laundry. A man who fell down a flight of stairs; I wasn't allowed to tend him." She paused and muttered to herself. "Mostly things like that. Ten or so patients. Three came in while I was there."

"Do you have any names?" Tik asked. "It's not like you to just see people as their injuries."

"I don't remember most of them," she said. "It was a bit cold and professional. It didn't feel like I could ask."

There were other reasons for the injuries she described. "I think we need to be careful tonight," Lena said. "Make sure we don't talk about the wrong thing or ask the wrong questions."

"You think those people are being punished?" Luis asked.

"The only thing missing is a woman who walked into an open door," she said.

"That wasn't missing," Mellow said. "She was discharged just after I got there. What do you mean?"

"Everything you mentioned, the injuries and the explanations, point to them being victims of abuse," Luis said.

Lena figured he'd seen his share of cases in his law practice. Before and after he was forced to be a gang lawyer.

"We could leave in ten minutes," Scott said. "All our stuff is here, and the gate is open."

That would put them on the road at night. The weather had cleared in the two days they'd been at Glass House, but the sun still set early. "No, I think we stay. Leave at first light. Just be careful. It's okay to watch for clues that show our assumption is right, but no trying to save anyone. We're too outnumbered."

The barracks they'd been assigned at the beginning was close to the entrance. Marnie had given them a set of bunk beds together and a large locker for their packs. Leaving was a matter of stuffing the few items they'd removed into the backpacks and walking across to the entrance. They didn't even need to let someone know they were going.

Shouting interrupted Lena's thoughts.

27

They ran to the door, stopping just inside to stay out of the incident until they knew what was happening.

"I guess we get to see how Marnie handles dissent," Tik said.

More than dissent, Lena thought.

The courtyard was filled with knots of people fighting. No weapons in evidence, but fists and feet were being used without consideration of the damage done.

Everything lit with a mixture of camp lanterns and fires. A disturbing blend of bright white and warm flickering yellow. It gave the scene a movie-like quality.

Except this wasn't entertainment. People went down bloody and now that the alarm was raised, the shouting stopped and the only sounds were thuds and cracks of broken bones.

"Isn't that one of the guards we saw the first day?" Mellow asked, pointing to a man who was attacking three others as if he did it regularly.

"I can't tell who's on which side," Lena said. "It's disorganized, and more people are coming."

Combatants flowed through the front entrance and the now sagging wagon gate. Others rushed from the main building. Everyone was dressed in similar clothes, but that didn't mean anything; no one had worn a uniform in the last two days.

"We need to grab our packs," Scott said. "If we have to leave, we need to go with everything. And if Marnie decides to lock the buildings down, we don't want to be caught inside."

"We might even get blamed," Luis said. "Unless this happens fairly often, it's a big coincidence that we show up just before someone attacks."

Scott returned to the doorway wearing his backpack and dragging two behind him. "I'll go get the others," he said. "Grab a knife, just in case."

Lena shrugged into her pack and then pulled the knife from its sheath on the side. New participants appeared from other buildings. So far it was all adults. The kids must be held somewhere safe.

"Watch out," Luis said as he grabbed Lena's pack and drew her to the side. "They're coming from the outlying tunnels. This isn't spontaneous. Someone planned it. Someone on the inside and on the outside. Look."

The farmers who'd run from behind the building separated to join the brawl. Lena started to identify the different sides now that there was more fighting. The attackers were pushing the defenders toward the main building. Most of the farmers joined the attackers, to her surprise.

Something ugly was hidden beneath the surface of Glass House. To arrange a mutiny in these times without fast and reliable communication was a difficult task. To turn insiders against their home was testament to how bad these secrets were.

"How do we get out?" Mellow asked.

While Lena watched the action, everyone in her group had prepped for escape. Knives held pointing down, ready to be used if needed.

"The fight is starting to shift toward the center," Luis said. "We can slip around the side. Try to get out without anyone noticing. Get back to the horses tonight."

"I wish we knew why," Mellow said. "Maybe this isn't about the community, or not about what they are doing. Maybe it's a raiding party. Maybe we should help."

"Hard to help when you don't know who the good guys are," Lena said. "Or maybe not the good guys, just the less bad guys."

"This isn't a raiding party," Luis said. "They'd come in hard. On horses, with blades, and no one on the inside joins the attackers. This fight is fueled by anger and resentment. Marnie made this possible, maybe even inevitable."

Tik led the way around the edges of the forecourt, hugging the shadows and watching the fight closely. The entrance to the little glass house was open, the panes trampled under foot and the frames bent with the force used to burst in.

Only a few more yards.

Lena held onto the rail of Scott's backpack with one hand. Mellow doing the same to Lena, forming a chain.

Ten more steps.

No one noticed them.

Five more steps.

A new fight broke out next to Lena. New combatants

ramming into two men who didn't have the sense to hug the walls in their attempt to get out.

Her hand pulled away from Scott's pack.

She felt a jolt as Mellow was knocked aside.

Lena switched her blade from her passive hold into a fighting grip. She widened her stance and tried to pick a target. The two hopeful escapees kept pushing against the new fighters. Lena shifted her feet again, maybe she didn't have to shed blood. She'd killed too many in the fight with the monks. She couldn't bring herself to stab anyone, no matter the side. If the two men were running, did it mean they weren't part of the problem here? Or were they trying to escape retribution?

Luis was right, this wasn't a raiding party.

She pushed her weight onto the balls of her feet and kicked out at the nearest knee. She made contact with enough force for one attacker to drop, but no sound of breaking.

The woman took out one of the escapees as she fell, then a mass tangle as the entire fight collapsed on the ground.

"Go," she said. "Just keep running, we'll stop when it's safe."

A scream tore through the crowd. Lena couldn't stop herself from looking toward the noise. Someone had drawn a weapon.

The center of the melee surged out like a rock had dropped in the middle of a pool as people stopped fighting to recoil from what happened.

The sharp metallic scent of blood filled the air.

"Marnie." The word ran through the crowd, growing louder by the second.

Did Marnie draw the knife, or was she bleeding out?

"Stop." A familiar voice shouted. "This was not why we came."

The crowd disagreed, and Lena feared their anger would turn on the person who was obviously behind the attack.

28

S omeone grabbed a lantern and held it high enough to light the scene in the center.

Astrid stood in all her Viking glory. Her left hand gripped around the arm of a girl who was holding a knife dripping with blood.

Marnie was already dead. No one could lose that much blood and live.

"She deserved it," the girl said, jerking her arm to release it. Astrid maintained her hold.

"Not before a trial," Astrid said. "Drop the blade."

The girl did as she was told.

"Anson, Ingrid, put her somewhere to cool off." The Astrid controlling the crowd was very different from the girl they'd rescued from Virtue, and even from the young warrior who'd followed Beattie toward Fort Revelation not that long ago.

"She can't see us," Scott said. "Let's give her time to sort this out before we say hi."

With the fighting over, Lena could see her friends beside

the entrance to the community. So close to getting out. But if they had managed, they wouldn't know Astrid was here. They wouldn't get a chance to talk to her.

"You all know what happened here," Astrid said to the crowd who was listening, probably in shock. "Only some of you know what happens outside. Everything Marnie did to keep Glass House safe would hurt others. She killed her own people if they disagreed with her or outlived their usefulness."

"Everyone contributes," a man called out. "That's the rule."

"Yeah," a woman said. "People who cause trouble put us all in danger."

"You'll have a chance to hear everything. One hour. In this building. Stories from anyone who wants to speak. Decisions on your future; ones that come from all of you. With the full picture."

She nodded to a few people in the crowd, and they started moving others to the main building, skirting Astrid, who was guarding Marnie's body. A few needed their wounds and injuries attended. They were carried into the same place.

"I'll go help," Mellow said. "You can catch me up on Astrid's news."

Lena stepped forward, motioning for the other three to stay behind. "Astrid."

She snapped her gaze to Lena. "What are you doing here?"

"Right back at you," Lena said.

"Well, that saves us a lot of work. Beattie and I were looking for you when we found out what was happening here. We can talk later. After these guys figure out what they want to do with their second chance."

"We'll wait inside, near the door." She waved Scott, Tik, and Luis forward. "Tik, keep an eye on Mellow."

"This could go very bad, very fast," Astrid said.

"What if you don't like their decision?" Lena asked.

"Not my problem. I hope they work something out. This place looks like it might be able to support everyone around. Just because an asshole got power doesn't mean they can't fix it."

Lena patted her arm and then went inside to wait with the others.

Minutes later, Astrid strode in and stepped onto the top of a table near the center of the floor.

"My people will leave in two hours. This is when you get to talk it out."

"You aren't taking over?" The question came from a woman in the middle of the crowd.

Astrid turned toward the sound of her voice. "No. We were traveling and met up with a few people that woman kicked out. They told us about an attack they were planning and why. We just helped them come up with a way to do it without slaughtering everyone."

"Marnie's dead," the same man who'd started the questions outside said.

"She should have been kept alive to answer for what she did. I guess she hurt the girl one too many times."

"How will we get along without Marnie?" a boy asked.

Lena noticed the crowd had shuffled into groups. The younger members were in the far corner, the farmers next and the livestock handlers on the other side. The attackers stayed together. Her attention was drawn by steps coming from the door. Sweeney was leading a small group of people with injuries.

Mellow was with them and talking to a woman. She

finished her conversation and joined Lena, pulling on her backpack in preparation to leave.

"The doctor," Mellow said. "She's going to talk to the crowd."

The doctor walked up to Astrid and said a few words. Astrid nodded and pulled the doctor up before returning to the floor. She strode toward Lena's group.

"Ready to go?" she asked.

"When you are," Scott said. "I'd like to hear this, first."

"I told them two hours. I need to stay in case they have questions. If you leave before me, wait just outside the gates."

Then the doctor started talking.

"I know you're worried. I was here at the beginning too, but things have changed. First of all, there are no hordes of bandits coming to take what we've grown. North of here is pretty empty. Mostly people who couldn't stick out the winter and went south."

"Why should we believe you?" a boy asked.

"I'll answer questions when I've finished talking," the doctor said. "Maybe you'll hear the answers in the story. You were told our allies are out there nearby. The truth is that Marnie kept them in need so they couldn't fight. Our supposed friends spend most of their time foraging for us. She paid them with the least amount of food she could get away with. Or did, I guess."

"How do you know this?" another man called out.

"I'm getting to that," the doctor said. "Most of you never got to see me in my official capacity. You'll get to hear from the people who did. But Marnie let me go looking for pharmaceutical supplies. Not me personally, but I had a team. They found all this out."

The crowd started murmuring. Lena tried to pick out words to test the attitude, but it was impossible.

"Who were they?" the first man asked.

"I wouldn't tell Marnie. I'm not telling you until we have some decisions made. Why did I do it? Because of Marnie. People who disagreed or didn't exactly fit her image of a good citizen ended up in my place." She waved the small group over. "I'll let them tell you what she did."

Sweeney joined the doctor on the table, struggling to get up there with the cast on his left arm from wrist to shoulder. "You know me," he said. "Been here forever, seems like. Someone told Marnie I was complaining. It doesn't matter if it was true or not. She took me to the top of the admin offices for a talk. That talk started with me getting a push that sent me down the stairs. Broken arm and elbow, some kind of damage to my shoulder. You think this will make me a better contributor? No, nor did she. I was going to be escorted out in the middle of the night."

The crowd went silent. Sweeney was a good choice for starting the recitation of abuse. These people knew him and didn't question his story. Each of the patients Mellow had treated followed. All with a similar story. It made Marnie sound like she was just looking for excuses to blow off steam by beating people up, like any abuser.

When the last person finished, the doctor started talking again. "That's the history. We need to move forward."

"With you leading?" the boy asked.

"Not interested," the doctor said. "I suggest we elect a council. We need to decide what kind of community we'll be."

After a moment, she turned to Astrid. "Do you have anything you want to say?"

"No."

The doctor turned to the crowd. "Are there any questions for the person who helped save us?"

When no one spoke up, Astrid said, "Then we'll be on our way. Good luck."

29

Beattie was waiting for them on a road halfway to the lake. Lena suggested any talk would be better around a campfire. So, they plodded through the night, Beattie and Astrid leading their horses to keep pace with the others who walked.

It didn't take much longer than the morning they'd gone to Glass House, but it felt longer. The emotional toll weighed on Lena like a second backpack full of rocks. The only good thing about leaving was, despite the darkness, it had only been early evening when the fight broke out. So, they would be back at camp before it was truly night.

Luis went to check the horses and lead Raven and Strider to empty stalls. Scott and Tik built the fire and started the tea. Within minutes, they were sitting around the flames and eager to talk.

"So, what happened?" Lena said. "Is Siren okay?"

Astrid looked at Beattie, and Lena feared the news was bad.

"You tell the story," Beattie said. "You need practice."

"Yeah, telling battle stories around the fire is a big thing for warriors, right?" Astrid laughed and raised her tea in acknowledgement of Beattie.

"The kid is fine. He's back with Nicolette and says he's never coming out again. She looked happy to have him, so I guess his story is done."

"There's more to life than this," Lena said. "His story goes on even now he's left us."

"Geez, Lena, I'm supposed to be practicing my story-telling. He's home and happy. That's it."

"No sadness that he will never get to Valhalla?" Beattie asked with a smile. "Vikings only go if they are killed in battle, right?"

"So literal. You want to tell it?"

"No, the stage is yours."

Their easy teasing was a good sign. Lena didn't think they'd be this casual if the reason they were back on the road was bad. The she realized someone would have to tell them about the monks. A chill shuddered through her at the idea Astrid would think it brave and honorable.

"It's not that long," Astrid said. "You heard the end of it at Glass House. We dropped off Siren first. Out of our way, but it was our responsibility. We got there without too much trouble. Ran into a few religious guys, but they left us alone after a while of preaching."

"You were lucky," Tik said. "We ran into them too. I'll tell you the details after you're done."

"Like I said, we dropped Siren off. Didn't go in this time. She didn't invite us, either. Did some hunting between the cult and the fort. Saw those kids, remember?"

"So, they managed," Lena said. "Did they remember you?"

She sipped her tea and nodded. "Seems they took on the role of advanced scouts for Greenly, not official, and he said they were more trouble than help. I think he liked the idea of keeping them safe and still out of the fort."

"Yeah," Beattie said. "He's thinking of setting up a camp with them, train them better. Give some of his team a chance at leadership."

"We stuck around a few days," Astrid said. She firmed her lips and paused for a long moment. "He appreciated the news. Pearl Two is a long way, so he figures they aren't his problem."

"I don't see Trixie going off the grid to take over a fort," Mellow said. "Or the gang getting anywhere if they try to take people. So, he's probably right. I hope he keeps the kids safe."

"It would be nice if he could form a..." Tik paused for thought. "I don't know, something like the old marshals. Kind of peacekeeping force."

"He's stuck in his ways," Astrid said. There was a heavy dollop of disdain in her voice. "We left. He said I couldn't join the fort. He offered Beattie that position, training the kids, said I could be there, too."

"Vikings aren't babysitters," Beattie said.

"Yup, that's what I said. Beattie just told him she was with me, and he'd lose her."

"So, you left?" His behavior was the same as most of the other leaders, the ones who hadn't tried to sell them off or use a community for abuse targets.

"I can always go back," Beattie said. "I don't want to."

"Did you notice how empty this area is?" Astrid said. "That doctor was right."

"Yes," Lena said. "I think she got the reason right, too. We'll see as we go farther south. If that's what we plan to do."

"Did you encounter problems on the road here?" Tik asked.

"Just empty towns." Beattie looked around at their camp. "We came mostly through the trails, so not too many of them either. We were hoping to find you, but if we didn't, we were going to head to Liberty. See what's going on."

"Get my revenge on Ivan," Astrid said.

"That's not likely to turn out well for anyone," Scott said.

"We'll see," Astrid said. "That guy is part of the gang. We can make it harder for them to operate. If the people we rescued are successful, maybe the world is a better place."

"Is that why you helped the people at Glass House?" Mellow asked.

"Letting assholes continue to be assholes isn't the right way to get the country back together," Beattie said. "We're not on a crusade, don't worry. Just, if we happen to run into a bad situation, we will try to make it less awful."

The conversation moved from subject to subject and Lena let the voices fade into the background as soon as Tik started to tell the monk story.

Is that my future? I can't imagine punishing people just because they didn't agree with me. Maybe that's not how it started with Marnie. Abuse wasn't always a male thing. Plenty of women were just plain mean.

Glass House was a good community, but somewhere it went wrong. Even if Marnie was always abusive, she somehow came into the leadership position. How would she have handled the challenges the farm faced? Marnie wouldn't have fought Newton Cole. She'd have found a way to use his men. She might have used violence against Poor-john's people.

Lena's thoughts turned to herself. If her people had

found Glass House when they'd fled New Surrey instead of heading for the farm, would it look different now?

She'd like to think the whole area would be prospering, but not knowing why the northern communities were abandoned, she couldn't be sure. The noise around the fire changed from conversation to action. They were preparing to settle in for the night.

"I'll take the first watch," Lena said. She needed more reflection time. Deep inside, she knew she wasn't capable of Marnie's actions, but she worried that the community would be just as bad without the woman. Was this world inevitably harsh? Was 'might is right' instead of cooperation the only option?

30

In the morning, Astrid pulled the maps out and spread them on the floor of the loft. Multiple maps would show them the whole distance home so they could work out timing, if it was necessary. Without any real need to investigate a specific area, choosing a destination seemed the best option to start.

"There's no way of knowing what's happening in these places," Mellow said. "I mean, is Boise abandoned too? Or Salt Lake City? Are we just exploring now, or still trying to figure a way to unite communities? They can't all be like Pearl Two or Glass House."

"I don't know how long we should keep looking for places to join alliances," Lena said. "There's a bunch of country between us and home, even if we head straight there. In the past, we'd have news or satellite photos to give us an idea of the conditions."

"It doesn't feel right to abandon the main reason we came," Scott said. "It was never going to be easy."

"Maybe it's too soon for big changes," Lena said. "You've

all told me that in one way or another. People are still in survival mode. That doesn't promote long term thinking."

"There's a compromise," Astrid said. "Yeah, before you say it, I'm capable of compromise. We could follow this route." She pointed to the main road. "Head south to see if we can find some people who've fled from the north. No one we helped came from there. How about in Glass House?"

"We didn't have time to get that close," Tik said. "You think there's a different reason than it was too hard to survive?"

"It's a lot of people," Beattie said. "Way more than could be taken in at Glass House. Even after the plagues."

"You think something bad happened?" Mellow asked.

Lena looked at the whole area on the map. "The towns in the hills were small tourist areas. After the plagues, probably less than a thousand remaining in the whole area. It doesn't explain Seattle or any of the bigger places, but maybe no one survived the first winter. The infrastructure could have broken down faster. It would only take one natural disaster to take out electricity. Or a single dam burst to take out the clean water. Some of these places would only have one or two survivors anyway."

"That's not enough," Beattie said. "The whole area we went through should have had around a thousand survivors."

"There are too many questions we might never answer," Luis said. "You didn't start this expedition with the idea of learning everything. You made decisions without any details all along. Step back and figure out what you want to learn."

Lena glanced at the map again, this time looking for what was there, not the answers. If the goal was still to be back at the farm by the end of the year, they couldn't go too far out of the way.

"If we pick a point too far south and east, we're on the road until next spring at least," she said. "When do you think people at home will start to worry?"

"They've been worried the entire time," Scott said. "By summer, they'll start to accept we're not coming back."

"I don't want them thinking we're dead," she said, "unless we are."

The others leaned over the map, muttering to themselves. Lena heard distances and other concerns being worked through by each of them alone. Their three new people didn't know exactly where the farm was, but close enough to join in calculating the best and worst timelines. This was going to take a while, and they definitely wanted to be out of the area today.

"I'll start getting stuff ready," she said. "I've seen enough of the map. I need to do some thinking."

What she meant was she didn't need to keep staring at the map with no idea of a purpose other than running home. She dragged all the items they'd unpacked while camping in the barn and repacked. When she was done, the others were talking together, so she started lowering the packs with one of their ropes. The ladder was attached, but straight down. Carrying a pack was a good way to fall off.

The horses were ready to go if their restlessness was any indication. She wiped them down and saddled them. This was the best way she'd found to let her mind work on a problem. The routine work and the soft snorts of the horses was like meditation.

She didn't want to head straight home. That realization was a weight lifted. It felt like running away to just abandon their purpose. Even if she didn't get her way and find potential allies, they needed to know about threats. The gangs were one, but she'd seen no sign of them at home. They were actually located in what used to be Canada, so maybe that explained it. The gangs were operating south, not north.

She had no idea what threats were closer to home. And if someone was out there, the farm needed to prepare defenses. Ignorance was too big a risk to take these days.

Lena hung the supply bags on Angel as she came to her decision. Time to rejoin the others.

"We think we should head back along the path we came," Scott said. "Check on what's happened in the time we were on the coast. Maybe just work out arrangements with the people who showed interest."

"Liberty and Beta?" Lena asked.

"Yeah. Mutual benefit there," Scott said.

"And I get to see Ivan again," Astrid said.

Lena let that go. Plenty of time to convince her how bad an idea it was to act on her anger while they rode.

"I've also been thinking that we need to know more about the threats," she said and then shared her idea of narrowing their southern path to encompass more of the land close to the farm. "Anything within a couple of months' travel. It gives us time to prepare."

"It will take us through Montana," Luis said. "I've been through there once or twice. It was pretty sparsely populated before. I can take us through some places that were good a couple of years ago."

"Then we head south," Tik said. "Turn up before we get as far as Boise. Be home for Christmas?"

"Unless there's a good reason not to," Lena said. "We're ready to ride."

As they were mounting up, Astrid pulled Lena aside. "I

think Beattie would like to settle at this farm. Is there room for us?"

Having two well-trained soldiers would be valuable, Lena thought. "I'll ask how the others feel about it."

Astrid nodded and took Raven's reins.

31

L ena's first instinct was to ask Luis if he wanted to come to the farm. To get the decisions all made at the same time. She held back because the request should come from him. What would happen if he said no? They had a long road ahead, and even though it felt like going home in the end was the right decision, there would be challenges to their progress.

She was ready to say yes to all of them. Luis would fill a role they currently didn't know they needed at home: storyteller. New stories, not just the same old retelling of their own history. There were plenty of communities around the farm if he still felt the need to wander. Or he could simply leave when he wanted to.

They were riding in pairs, well, if Angel counted. Astrid and Beattie led them, for once not taking front and rear guard. She rode with Scott, Tik and Mellow just ahead, Luis and Angel trailing. A good time to talk without being overheard. She thought the decision should be made, not secretly, but definitely privately.

"Astrid and Beattie want to move into the farm," she said to Scott. "What do you think?"

"Surprised, and not surprised, really. They need a home, and the last one rejected them. You think they'll fit in the house? No one there has their skills."

"I'm hoping the barracks extension has been done," Lena said. "Unless someone has moved on while we explored, the house is full."

"We can build a cabin pretty fast," he said. "Just a bedroom and living room. They can use the house for everything else."

"So, you're okay with it?" Lena hoped he'd give her more reason than just because they traveled together. The ghost of her fear of turning into Marnie, not the cruelty part, but the position of leader in a growing community, had her second guessing everything. They didn't have room to take in everyone. And other than Pallavi and Mahir, they hadn't up to the time she left. A year could have changed a lot.

"I think they will be worth the short inconvenience of making room. The farm needs fresh faces. The whole alliance needs an organized force. Not just the scattered fighters. Seems like a dream match."

What she'd learned the most on this trip was that every community needed some kind of protection. Not just farmers or crafters pulled together in a crisis. Trained people who would patrol, get ahead of any threat. Those who would pass on skills so everyone was ready to fight for their home.

"I'm not sure if they want to do that," she said, "or maybe they'll create that sort of peacekeeper force Tik talked about. A problem for the future, though. Okay, I'll talk to Mellow and Tik later today."

The traveling was smoother than before. The weather wasn't as cold. It rained, but the edge of sleet or snow was gone. Being wet was never something Lena wished for, but at least they could keep going without the worry of hypothermia. And the rain cleaned off the foliage enough to release a pine scent, which seemed to perk everyone up from their quiet reflection.

Another abandoned rest area worked for their midday stop. Scott and Luis took the horses to a pond for water, and Beattie sent Astrid to scout the area. "I think we were being watched," she said. "Just the last hour. I'm going to return on foot, see if I can settle my mind. Maybe find the watchers, or proof it was just a creepy feeling. I'll be back within an hour."

Lena had felt it too, but glancing to the side hadn't given her any clues. At least it wasn't paranoia. And voicing it on the road was probably a bad idea. If they were being stalked, the danger wouldn't go away; it would just get more stealthy.

As if it had been planned, Lena was left setting up for lunch with Tik and Mellow. At that thought, she realized it probably had been orchestrated. Good. It let her deal with any objections. She wasn't sure if the vote needed to be unanimous or a majority. Of if she should be the one making the rules.

She told Mellow and Tik about the request. "Beattie didn't ask me herself. I guess I trust Astrid not to lie about this."

"I was trying to figure out what changed with her," Tik said. "Yeah, the fighting skills have become second nature, but it's the lying. Remember at the beginning? She would tell you the sky is green just for something to do."

"You're right," Lena said. "I don't think she's done that

once in the last day. I guess that's a point to her. And to Beattie, because she must have made it happen."

The kettle was boiling over the fire. Lena poured it over the tea leaves and set it to steep.

"I don't know if she'll be happy," Mellow said. "The farm isn't exciting. What if she decides to make things happen to avoid boredom?"

"That's where her Viking genes can be used in our favor," Lena said. "When they weren't fighting, they were farmers and craftsmen, fishermen, everything."

"And there's nothing to stop her and Beattie exploring," Tik said. "I'd feel better if either of them went with the next group of people who get itchy feet. I don't want us to just hole up at home and hope for the best. We should check on the city people, and Poorjohn's. I didn't like just leaving them to fend for themselves."

They'd settled around Calgary, and if anyone knew more about the gangs operating between the two old countries, it could be the groups newly settled in the area. A small voice wondered if the source of the problems came from the refugees they'd sent away from the farm. That the town refugees were the gang.

"So, are you okay if I say yes?" she asked.

"We need them as much as they need us," Tik said. "So yes."

"Mellow? You haven't said much. Do you have more worries?" Lena knew Mellow would think through the implications before giving her an answer. She hoped it wouldn't take days.

"I think Maya and Jason would be thrilled," Mellow said. "I'm not sure if the other communities will be happy for us to have professional fighters. You'd need to explain the situation fast."

"And we need to know what Beattie and Astrid expect to do. Maybe they'll want to retire."

Mellow laughed at the idea of the two warriors sitting the action out.

"I guess I'm happy to give them the opportunity to try living with us. Maybe in the end they'll decide to move on."

32

Beattie returned by the time Lena was cleaning the teapot and mugs.

"Anything?" Lena asked.

"A cougar," Beattie said. "Pretty hungry if he was willing to try for one of our horses. But I guess they look worth it when we settle for the night."

"Do we need to put a closer watch?" If we found any more threats, no one would get any sleep until they were inside a community's protection.

"I scared it off," Beattie said. "If it stops trailing us, it will find plenty of game or fish. I think we need to set someone in with the horses if we sleep outside. Bears will be coming out of hibernation soon. Horses look like an easy meal."

"We'll try for covered camps," Lena said. "Did Astrid tell you she asked to move in with us at the farm?"

"No, but we talked about it," Beattie said. "She's still learning patience."

"You are both welcome," Lena said. "Do you want to tell her?"

"I think you should. She'll be really happy. Maybe it will take her mind off revenge."

Astrid was delighted, as if she'd expected rejection or a lot of conditions. The ride to where they would spend the night was chattier than before. And the girl hustled to set up the camp.

Lena noticed little changes as they talked about setting more guards because of animals. Astrid acted as though Luis was a servant. Nothing overt, and Luis didn't say anything. But the girl clearly saw him as an outsider.

"Astrid," Lena said, "please go take care of the horses. And I think you should sit the first watch with them. Make sure no other animals are looking for a meal."

"Luis usually does that," she said. "I can watch over the people. I can sit more than one watch if you want."

"I think it would be good for you to do it tonight," Lena said. "We're all on the same team here. We all share the load."

Astrid looked stunned, as if Lena had taken away her invitation. She glanced toward Beattie, who was looking for dry tinder and kindling. Lena couldn't help thinking Beattie was ignoring them on purpose. Perhaps to teach Astrid that she couldn't avoid taking orders from anyone.

"Does that mean Tik and Mellow will sit with the horses too?" she finally said.

Lena could see the battle of emotions play across Astrid's face. "Yes. Me too. Why do you need to ask?"

She scowled, and Lena started to ask why when the girl gave a huff. Her emotions flipped from annoyance to acceptance in an instant. The scowl had been directed internally. She did learn fast.

"Okay. I guess I understand why the rules changed when we became part of the family," she said.

"The rules didn't change, Astrid." Beattie said as she dropped the handful of twigs and bark next to the fire.

Astrid turned and went to settle the horses in the trees, close enough together that they could be watched. If any threat approached, the animals would show their alarm. Having a human with them might discourage even the hungriest animal.

"She won't be able to get away with that attitude at the farm," Lena said.

"We have plenty of time to hone her social skills," Beattie said as she made a pyramid of wood for the fire. "Remember, she hasn't had a home since she was a kid. And she's a teenager. They come with attitude in buckets. I'll keep her from pissing anyone off too much."

Beattie was barely an adult herself. Her assessment of Astrid brought a smile to Lena until she thought about the kids she'd left behind. Maya and Jason would be teenagers, or close enough. Mahir was only a year behind Maya. Was Ava dealing with three sassy kids?

"You don't have to do it alone," Lena said. "I think we all need to be on the lookout for her. If she tries too hard to suppress the emotions, they might turn into something darker."

"I forgot we're a team," Beattie said. "I guess Greenly sending us away hurt me more than I thought."

The next morning, the southern leg of their trip would end. Turning north and leaving the side roads for the forest paths would slow them down, but it would be safer.

The feeling of being watched hadn't abated despite Beattie's discovery of the cougar.

"There are too many little towns and camps around here," Beattie said. "For all we know, it's not just one person. They could be changing out as we pass some unmarked territory. I think if we keep moving, we won't rise to the level of a threat. Whoever it is will just watch to make sure we don't try to move in."

"I hope it ends soon," Lena said. "Traveling for days with my skin crawling is going to be hell."

"The forest was fine when we came out from Fort Revelation," Astrid said, reaching for a handful of moss hanging from a branch to dry for the night's fire. "No threats from humans or animals."

"We'll cross the river early if we can find a bridge," Scott said. "Should drop any followers. If not, we'll do it outside Banks. There's a town called Crouch a bit farther in. We should make it by tomorrow night."

33

The next night they approached Crouch from the opposite side of the river to a vantage point high enough to check the town for danger before entering or moving on. If something looked worth exploring, it was an easy trip back across the small bridge. Much smaller than the one they'd used earlier in the day. If they sensed anything wrong in the town, the forest was within steps.

"I talked to Astrid," Beattie said as she stood with Lena, holding the horses.

"How did it go?" Lena asked quietly. Astrid was climbing up the rocks on the side of the road to get a better look at the town. There was very little privacy on the road, so if Astrid had done the typical yelling about not being a kid, Lena would have known.

"I told her she was creating a division. That a warrior who couldn't accept her companions as equals, no matter who they were, would not live long. She said she knew and to get off her back."

"Ah. Well, I think it will work," Lena said. "She takes her

warrior behavior very seriously. I've noticed she sometimes reacts like she's not listening when she's actually trying to process it through her 'how to be a Viking' assumptions."

Beattie chuckled. "Yeah, I'm not looking forward to a time when she decides she knows enough about being a Viking that she can stop adapting. I'll have to find some other way to get through her stubborn head."

"At the farm there's a lot of help," Lena said. "No one takes any attitude. And we have some actual mothers. They seem to know exactly how to deal with attitude."

"There are people in the town," Scott said, lowering his binoculars. "I think it makes sense for a few of us to go in."

"Does it look like I might run into trouble?" Lena asked. "I just want a conversation, not even an overnight stay. We need to keep moving."

"Some have guns, but we all know it doesn't mean they have ammunition," Astrid said, joining them on the tarmac. "You want to go in looking non-threatening?"

"It's probably the best," Lena said. "If we go in bristling with weapons, it's hard to get people to trust us enough to talk." Was Astrid pushing for a fight?

"Okay," Astrid said. "You, Mellow and Luis. The rest of us can watch from up here. Try to stay outside. We can be there in a few minutes if something goes wrong."

The contrast between the beginning of their journey and now was startling. She remembered walking up to community gates without much preparation. Not completely blind to the dangers, but optimistic. Now, she was taking advice from a warrior. Worried more about trouble than getting information. Even thinking about an escape plan rather than how to engage in a conversation.

"Gates?" she asked.

"No. Just guards at the bridge," Tik said. "No one came

or went while we watched. Astrid's plan is sound. Take your horses."

"So we can get out fast?" Luis asked. "We should take some of the supplies, too. Travelers don't just wander around on horseback."

"No, but scouts for a raiding party might," Beattie said. "Are we just going to stand around until it gets dark?"

"Okay, stay outside, get out fast," Lena said. "Are we sure it's worth even going?"

"No." Scott's answer surprised Lena. "So far, we haven't gotten much more than trouble. But we'll regret it if we don't. This is probably the last chance before we hit Liberty."

Lena mounted and waited for Luis and Mellow to join her. They rode down the approach to the bridge. It was little more than an extension of the road at this point. She refused to look back and give the guards notice that people were watching.

There were three of them, two women and one man. The oldest woman was standing in the middle of the bridge deck, ready to turn visitors around if necessary. The younger woman looked barely out of her teens, and the man could have been her father.

"What's your business?" the woman in the center asked. She stepped forward and the other two moved closer. They all carried rifles, not so great at close range, even if they had ammunition.

"Passing through," Lena said. "Hoping for some local news."

"Just you three?" she asked.

This could be a trick. No one had taken particular care to remain hidden when they used their binoculars. There was more than a slim chance that this woman knew someone watched them. Lena thought of lying but decided to share the truth instead. How could she expect these strangers to trust them if she started with a lie?

"Some of us stayed up in the hills," she said. "Didn't want to seem like we were dangerous. If we can talk to whoever knows the most around here, we'll head out right after."

The woman stared at Lena, ignoring Luis and Mellow. Then she gave a short nod and said, "Bella, go get Ike. Be quick."

Lena stayed mounted. If this Ike gave them permission to get down, she'd do so. If this was a trap, she wouldn't risk the time it took to remount.

A few silent minutes later, a man followed Bella back to the bridge. He was young, maybe mid-twenties.

"You wanted to chat?" he asked, his voice warm and rich. "You start."

"Are you in charge here?" Lena asked.

"Why?"

"Some questions can only be answered by a leader. I don't want to waste anyone's time."

"You got a name? Who are those two?"

Lena introduced them. "It looks like most of the people northwest of here are gone. Do you know why?"

"To the point. Good, we all got more important things to do. As I heard it, they were hit bad by the sickness, then the survivalists hit them hard. Took their supplies, killed them."

"How true do you think that is?"

Ike started to glance behind him toward the guards but caught himself. He stared at Lena as he spoke, "Got a few of the survivors living here. So true enough. What do you really want?"

The sense of being unwelcome went from mild suspicion to a brick wall. "I guess two things," Lena said. "How are you thriving?"

"Trouble with the survivalists didn't get this far. Not a lot of them around. We didn't wait until it was over to put protections in place."

"We're not here to take anything," Mellow said. "Just information."

"Doesn't matter why you're here," Ike said. "What's the other thing?"

It seemed useless at this point to bring up her dream, but she would regret it if she didn't, and maybe unity would come from unexpected places. "I'm wondering if the country is ready for some alliances. Maybe get us back to when we could trust people again?"

Ike burst out laughing. "You have anyone say sure?"

"Not yet," Lena said. "A few people interested but not ready to commit."

"I don't trust anyone I can't look in the eye," Ike said. "You go along now. There's a bunch of campsites around no one's claimed yet." He turned and walked away. The guards raised their rifles, but didn't aim at anyone.

"We're going," Luis said.

34

—————

Campsite signs pointed them toward the woods on either side of the road for the rest of the day. Lena hadn't wanted to follow Ike's advice in case there was a trap set up. He might have said they'd be safe, or at least hinted at it, but she wasn't naive enough to take him at his word. He could have allies outside waiting to take everything from them, including their lives. Or he might be telling the truth. Either way, she wasn't going to hang around.

They'd left the area immediately, riding in silence for the afternoon, saving the details of their conversation until they settled.

Their shelter was a gas station again. Lena's gut churned at the memory of the slaughter at their last stop, but she pushed it aside. The battle was awful, but they'd stayed in a lot of these places without trouble before. And it was that or under the stars.

It was the usual layout. A handful of pumps and a general store, this time. In the hills, this might have been the only place to get groceries before.

"We can stay in the store section," Tik said. "There's a back entrance that we can block. And the contents are long gone. No one around here will come scavenging."

"We keep double watch," Beattie said. "While it's light, we can eat together, but when the sun goes down, we keep it to a couple of those flashlights."

The last people who'd come to the station and taken the supplies had been kind enough to shut the doors when they left. Vermin didn't need open doors, but the lack of debris meant they didn't nest. The smell was bearable.

"Set the fire outside," Scott said. "There's not enough ventilation in here. And I don't smell fumes in the forecourt."

Lena listened to the preparations while she unpacked the food they'd prepare for dinner. The last of the canned food, not enough of one kind to call a meal, but they'd all get a taste of each. Stew, canned corn, chili, and some pasta in sauce. Enough of each to fill their bellies. Then tomorrow, back on dried everything.

"You can tell us the details of your discussion over dinner," Tik said. "It didn't look like they were interested in welcoming us in for a few days. Or like they were going to attack."

"That about sums it up," Mellow said. She put pans on the counter and handed Lena a can opener. "What did those guards do after we left?"

"They watched you until you got to the trees," Astrid said. "Making sure you were really going. Give me the lighter and I'll get the fire going."

AN HOUR LATER, as the sun dropped lower in the sky, they sat around the fire, which had been set up just far enough from the tanks to avoid a fire. Lena didn't smell gas. Scott was right, no combustible fuel, but she didn't want to take chances.

"So that's the story about why so many people are gone," Mellow said as she finished telling what happened in Crouch. "I guess it makes some kind of awful sense."

"Did you believe him?" Beattie asked. "About them being safe because they didn't have survivalists?"

"You notice he didn't want to answer how he knew?" Luis said. "I'm guessing that was not quite the truth. These mountains are exactly the place those preppers would use."

"He was lying," Lena said. "I just don't know what about or why."

"I think that town is full of the people who would have set up in the mountains," Mellow said. "They just found the houses in town a lot more comfortable. And maybe his people took part in the raids. I'll bet he knows firsthand what happened."

"If that's true, we need to be more careful," Beattie said. "We aren't going to stick around for a leisurely breakfast tomorrow."

Astrid stood and strolled toward the parking lot with the empty cans in a cardboard box, like she was disposing of the garbage. Lena watched her approach the bushes that hid the dumpster they'd noticed earlier.

She dropped the box and reached into the bushes like a viper striking. Someone screeched in anger and Astrid pulled the young girl who'd been guarding the bridge at Crouch out into the light.

"Are you alone?" Astrid asked calmly. The words sounded more menacing than if she'd yelled.

"Yes. I got sent out to make sure you're moving on."

Lena stood and joined Astrid. "Your name?" She'd heard the guard say it, but couldn't remember.

"You don't need it," the girl said.

"Why are you here?"

"Told you."

"Astrid, you, Beattie, and Tik go check to see if she's lying about being alone," Lena said.

She took control of the girl and urged her toward the fire. The three she'd sent on recon were silent as they slipped into the shadows.

"What are you going to do with me?" the girl asked.

"Are you hungry?" Mellow asked.

"No, got my own supplies."

"Do you have a horse?" Scott asked.

"How else would I keep close?"

"You heard us talking," Lena said. "Were we right?"

She pressed her lips together to keep her answers inside.

"We aren't interested in your community," Lena said. "Why not tell us?"

"Don't trust anyone."

"Is that the motto? Or just Ike's instructions?" Lena worried about how they'd get rid of this problem. Not permanently, but surely she wasn't going to follow them for much longer.

"Doesn't matter. I heard you. Maybe you got some of it right. Are you going to kill me?"

"No. Are you going to go back to Ike? Or should we be worried about an attack?" Scott asked.

"Like I said, just want to make sure you're moving on," the girl said.

Tik returned leading a horse. "Yours?" he asked.

"No one owns him. He's for all of us."

"Fine. I guess we'll just set him free then." Tik walked away, holding the reins.

"How am I supposed to get back on foot?"

"It's only a day or so walk," Lena said, "or you can keep the ride. There's no point in letting him stumble around here and break a leg. We're not stupid. We will be looking out for you tomorrow. If you keep following us, we'll take the horse and send you home with a message."

"Let me go now," she said. "I know the trails. I can get there by morning. I don't care what you do. If you come back to Crouch, we'll deal with you."

Lena called Tik back. "When the others get back with their report, we'll send her home. You can follow her for a while, right?"

Beattie led Astrid out of the trees at that moment. "No one else around. We'll escort her far enough. Set up the watch."

"What happened?" Mellow stepped forward to take Beattie's hand. "This is bleeding. Did you wash it?"

"A scratch. I know better than to clean a wound in a stream." Beattie pulled her hand away.

"That's not a scratch," Astrid said, grabbing her wrist. "How did you hide this from me?"

"It just happened. Let Mellow treat it and we can go to bed after we escort our little spy."

"Tik will do that," Mellow said. "Come inside."

35

Lena and Mellow stood the last watch and, as the sun bleached the sky, both stood and shook out their stiff joints. Sitting outside gave them the advantage of seeing anyone approaching before it was too late. It also meant they were in the weather. Even with no snow or rain, it was bitterly cold in the mountains.

"If there was going to be trouble, it would have come by now," Mellow said.

"That's what I was just thinking. We'll get another day between us and Crouch before we'll feel comfortable."

Mellow brushed the dirt from the seat of her pants. "I'll check on Beattie."

Lena shifted the half-burned wood from last night's fire to the side and started building the last of the tinder and kindling into a pile. A hot breakfast would do more than anything else to get them ready for a long ride.

Mellow leaned through the open door and called her name.

"Something wrong?" She turned to look, and her answer was written all over Mellow's face. "How bad?"

"Beattie. That wound is infected. She's got a fever. Can you brew some willow bark tea?"

"For the fever, sure, but we don't have any antibiotics. Is she going to be okay?"

"We shouldn't ride out today," Mellow said. "Let's get her comfortable and Astrid calmed down. There are a few natural treatments. I just need to figure out which ones we can find here."

"Send Astrid out to me and I'll keep her occupied."

Lena took one of the water jugs from the pile of sacks near the door. They'd stopped to fill the containers yesterday and had boiled the water to make it safe. Inside Mellow's saddlebag was the small cache of medicinal supplies. She pulled out the individually labeled packages and set the willow bark to the side before searching the other labels. Feverfew and witch hazel might help the infection. Finally, she reached in for the bandages and pads Mellow had taken from the clinic in Pearl Two.

"Mellow said make the tea strong." Astrid was standing over the fire, feeding it bits and pieces of fuel to get it started.

"Get the water boiling," Lena said. "I'm going to take these to her."

Astrid looked up from the flames. "Is she going to be okay?"

"Mellow is good at healing people," Lena said. "I think Beattie will recover. I don't know how long it will take."

"She'll be pissed if she can't fight."

"That makes you field commander." Lena restored the remaining medical supplies and stood. "Is that the right rank?"

Astrid fought the smile that tried to form. "I'd rather she was better."

"Think good thoughts," Lena said. "What would your Viking ancestors do?"

"Probably sacrifice an animal to the god in charge." The smile won out. "They were assholes."

"I'll be back in a second." She slipped into the store to see Mellow talking to Beattie, who was propped up against the wall. Tik and Scott were making plans with Luis in the corner.

"The fire will be ready soon to make the tea," Lena said. "How's the patient?"

"Ready to ride," Beattie said, her voice weak.

"No, you are not," Mellow said. "We're resting today so you can ride tomorrow. And you will follow my orders until I say you are healed."

Beattie blinked and then gave Mellow a mock glare. "Yes, ma'am. How's Astrid?"

"Ready to chop down the forest to punish the tree," Lena said. There was no benefit in telling Beattie that Astrid was already mourning her. "Will either of these help?" She handed Mellow the feverfew and witch hazel.

"Add a pinch of the feverfew to the tea and soak the witch hazel. We can use that to clean the wound."

THE TEA DIDN'T DO much to reduce the fever, but soon after drinking it, Beattie fell asleep. Lena helped Mellow clean and wrap the wound before she looked around. The others were outside the store, giving them privacy.

"It's bad, right?" Lena asked. "How much does Astrid know?"

Mellow picked up the soiled gauze pads and then moved away from the sleeping patient. "Beattie sent her out before I started checking her. She asked me to keep Astrid positive about healing. She actually said, 'if I have to keep worrying about her, I won't be able to rest.'"

"It's odd how we forget death can come from such simple things these days." Lena knew exactly what Mellow was going to suggest in the extreme chance the infection spread. "Let's see what comes of this rest."

Outside, Astrid stood when Lena and Mellow came to the fire. "Can I sit with her? Is she going to be okay?"

"Beattie is sleeping," Lena said. "She needs rest, so don't wake her up."

The girl ran inside the store.

Scott handed Lena and Mellow bowls. "Breakfast. I guess we'll camp here for a while."

"A day," Mellow said. "We'll know more this evening. If she's improving, we might be able to move on. If not... let's leave that until we have more information."

"We could hunt," Luis said. "And to be honest, since we left Glass House, we've all been strung tight. A day or two here is not that bad an idea."

"Gives a chance for the weather to improve," Scott said. "It's not like we have a schedule. And that girl will tell Ike we're moving on."

Lena finished her oatmeal and put the bowl on the ground. "We need to make this a more usable camp. Clean out the store. Maybe the toilet will work like that other place. Set up watches during the day. It's only us five. Astrid isn't going to leave Beattie until she's healed."

LUIS AND SCOTT headed out after they'd cleaned up and checked what could be done to make them more comfortable. They were looking for good places to observe their surroundings. And set a few traps for small game.

Astrid commandeered the sleeping bags to form a nest for Beattie. Lena made a broom from some fir branches and swept the dust gently away. The toilet didn't work, but it did have a first aid kit tucked into a cabinet. Mellow used the supplies to clean the wound again while Beattie continued to sleep.

"It's not better," she whispered to Lena later as they fed the horses. "Not worse either, but it can't stay like it is."

"Worse case?" Lena asked.

"Amputation. That comes with all kinds of complications." Mellow wrapped her arms around her body. "Including the fact I have no idea how to do it or if I can in the end."

"When will we know?" Lena thought through all the sharp implements. "If it comes to cutting her hand off, I can do it. Remember how Deb taught us to dress a deer?"

"I'd completely forgotten. We'd go for the joint right? Wrist?"

Lena closed her eyes. Trying to tell herself it was the same didn't help. Beattie was her friend, not a dead animal. "The elbow is probably smarter."

"She won't be able to fight," Mellow said.

"We'll deal with that later," Lena said, feeling queasy despite trying to sound professional. "There's always a way around if someone is determined. If we have to do it, we'll use the ax. We can clean it in the fire and I kept some of the alcohol wipes to sterilize it."

"Astrid? Someone will need to hold her back." Mellow wiped at her eyes to clear the tears forming.

"She might want to do it," Lena said. "And maybe that's the best option for her to heal beyond the surgery."

36

Through the night, they'd all taken turns sitting with Beattie and Astrid. Lena worried that they were spread too thin as she sat her turn watching the two women. Mellow was sleeping close by, ready to be woken if anything changed. Scott and Tik were sitting guard outside, and Luis was pretending to sleep not far away.

Tomorrow they would be too tired to move on no matter what happened. It would be better for Beattie to rest longer, but no guarantee anyone would rest until they were on their way. If she had a choice, Lena would never stay in a gas station again.

Beattie moaned, and Astrid leaned in to check her temperature. "It's the same," she said. "That's good, right? At least it's not worse."

"The treatments take a while," Lena said. There was no point in continuing with her thoughts that in the old days, Beattie would be walking around fine by now. Antibiotics were a thing of the past and likely wouldn't come back for longer than her lifetime. "You should try to sleep. I'll wake you if something happens."

"I'm not tired."

"You can barely keep your eyes open," Lena said. "We need you rested. Beattie needs you at a hundred percent. You'll be our only warrior because when the infection goes, she'll still be weak."

Astrid stared at Lena in defiance until it was broken by a yawn. "Fine, but I'm not moving from her side." She slid down to lay on the bare floor and, despite her words, was asleep before she'd taken two breaths.

Lena took Beattie's hand and turned it over to look under the wrappings. The wound was swollen and puffy. A crust of yellow filled the edges. Scabbing was good, right? There was no sign of red lines, which meant the infection wasn't spreading.

As much as she wanted the wound to heal, that yellow crust meant it was covering the infection and it would get worse. Before it sealed, the wound needed to be clean of anything that could kill Beattie.

Lena removed the bandage and gauze pad. Beattie moaned again. "Shh, it's okay," Lena murmured. A glance at Astrid reassured her that the girl was still asleep.

Lifting the cover on the bowl of herbal antiseptic, Lena gently cleaned the area, glad to see healthy skin. No need for the ax unless things got worse.

"Here," Luis whispered. "I just remembered we got some unguent from that Costco. Forgot to add it to the medical supplies when we left. It'll keep things from getting tight. She'll appreciate it when she's trying to get her full range of motion back."

The Costco was their last successful scavenge. Lena took the tin and opened it, the sharp scent of rosemary and lemon hitting her nose. "We have time to reorganize all our supplies. Tomorrow, we'll do that while we rest."

"That looks clean," he said, nodding toward Beattie's hand. "Underneath the mess."

"I hope it's a good sign," Lena said. "We'll ask Mellow in the morning. Her fever isn't breaking. What if there's a secondary infection?"

"Fever might be helping her fight," Luis said. He reached and touched the back of his hand to Beattie's forehead. "Not dangerously high. Just enough to sap her strength."

"Go get some actual sleep," Lena said. "I'll put some of this on the gauze pad when I wrap it back up."

"Put some on and let it breathe for a bit," Luis said. He went back to his patch on the floor.

THE SUN WAS COMING up when Scott and Tik entered. "There's nothing out there," Scott said. "We took turns ranging out all night."

"I'll start breakfast," Lena said, pushing herself up from the floor.

"You've been up all night," Scott said. "We'll take care of everything."

"You have, too. Are you saying I'm too old to survive a night on a hard floor?"

He pulled her close and kissed her. "Yes."

She swatted his arm and went to talk to Mellow.

"What can we do about the fever?" Lena asked.

"There's nothing more," Mellow said. "If the wound is healing, then we just have to wait for the fever to break."

Lena showed her the wound. Astrid stirred and sat up to keep a close eye on them.

"She's thrown off the infection," Mellow said. "That balm will help a lot; the rosemary might clear out the last of it. I forgot about the stuff we got from the Costco pharmacy, too. Lots of first aid stuff, if I remember right."

Beattie shifted and opened her eyes. "So, I lived through the night?" Her voice was dry and weak.

"You did." Astrid bent down to give her an awkward hug. "She's sweating."

"Fever's broken," Mellow said.

Beattie tried to stand. She was too weak to do more than sit up. "We can head out soon," she said. "Just need a bit of food."

Mellow pushed her back down. "No. Rest and food, and water. We all need a break. If this place is safe, we should hang around for a day or two."

"Fine," Beattie said. "If you all need a rest, we can stick around."

37

They stayed in the gas station for two more days. Beattie finally admitted on day two that she wasn't at a hundred percent. Mellow took that as a victory, and a sign her patient would take it easy.

The time wasn't wasted during their forced stop. When they knew they were staying for more than a day, everyone emptied their packs and all the saddle bags. When everything was laid out on a clean portion of the floor, it was clear the ointment wasn't the only thing everyone forgot.

"Can we make a list?" Mellow asked. "And organize it better. Make it easier to grab what we need. Like packs of gauze and ointment for injuries?"

"I almost forgot we'd stopped there," Lena said. "Some of the stuff we pulled off the shelves in that Costco could have helped earlier."

She checked the expiry dates on the tubes of medicinal creams and remembered questioning if they still worked. "We should never have forgotten this," she said.

"Lots happened, and we're used to not having things,

"Luis said. "It's not like anyone died. This was the first time we needed anything for more than a scratch."

The trees grew thicker as they moved away from the road. No humans logging or cutting wood for fires in the last years had left nature to fill the space.

Birds flew up from undergrowth at the sound of the horses. A few early mosquitoes whined around Lena's head. The occasional sound of twigs snapping reminded them that humans and horses weren't the only four-footed animals around. Being in the trees let Lena forget the emptiness of the whole area.

"Do you want to look for settlements?" Scott asked. "There aren't any towns, but there must be some camps people have populated."

Lena didn't answer right away. If she'd lost her belief in a better future, was there any point in looking for allies? "You think that someone who built a community in here will want to be part of something bigger?"

"You thought Greenly would," he said. "Why not here?"

"I guess I figured they would all be hill people," she said. "Hiding out on purpose. Ready to shoot first and never ask questions."

"Cannibals?" He laughed.

"Okay. I guess I've got my prejudices, too."

They rode on, Beattie now staying behind Astrid rather in the front. Lena scanned the trees on the sides of the hiking path for signs of occupation while she mulled over Scott's suggestions.

It wasn't just her assumption about the type of people who would retreat to the woods in a crisis. Keith had been planning to do that way back in New Surrey when she asked him to join her on the trek to her aunt's farm.

She'd been filled with doubt since they learned what

Trixie was up to. The events at Glass House hurt more than she thought because they reinforced her lack of success. It wasn't that the leaders were both women. Lena had never been one to believe the cultural assumption that women wouldn't do evil like men. It was the casual way both went about it.

Is that why I'm happy to rush home?

"I guess we should take a look," she said to Scott as they dismounted for a meal. "We'll never know if there are good people out here if we don't keep searching, right?"

As they stood eating the jerky and dried fruit they'd put aside for lunch, Lena asked the others what they thought.

"Beattie isn't ready to do that," Astrid said. "She can't defend us until she's healed."

"I can speak for myself," Beattie snapped the words out.

The calm, professional veneer had cracked an hour into the ride. The pain in her hand and Astrid's constant mothering were too much for her.

Lena sympathized. Having your sense of value taken away was shocking. Mellow said Beattie would heal completely. Lena hoped it was quick enough that the relationship between Astrid and Beattie didn't suffer.

"So, what do you all think?" she asked. "Do we sidetrack a bit or just keep moving on?"

"We're going pretty slow right now," Tik said. "It wouldn't hurt for us to scout. Me and Astrid should be enough."

And that would give Beattie some peace, Lena thought.

"I'm not going anywhere," Astrid said. "Beattie needs me."

"You will scout," Beattie said. "We need to know the dangers and until I am fit, you are the best scout and fighter. I will not die in your absence."

The glare Astrid gave her was pure teenager. "Fine."

"Let's get the horses watered," Luis said. "The two of you can go on foot for a bit. I'm not sure riding is a good tactic for a sneaky look."

Astrid tossed Raven's reins to Luis and gave Tik a pointed look when he took his time.

"We'll go for ten minutes," she said. "We'll decide what is best."

Lena watched as they slipped between two trees and disappeared.

"Ten minutes doesn't seem like enough," Mellow said.

"Ten minutes of peace sounds like heaven," Beattie said. "And it's plenty to check the terrain. If they go on foot, we'll have to ride slow and still wait for them when we stop."

"Astrid is worried about you," Lena said.

"I know. Worrying isn't helping anyone. She's worn out with imaginary situations, and I'm feeling guilty for putting her in that position. She needs to learn to channel her fears into productive actions," Beattie said. She pulled her hand into her body and held it there. "This is just an injury. I'll survive."

Mellow walked over to them with the antiseptic cream in her hand. "Time to check it," she said. "And you can't keep it curled like that. You don't want the tendons to shrink."

"It's barely closed," Beattie said.

"It doesn't take long," Mellow said.

"You know, I was hoping not to be fussed over for a few minutes," Beattie said, then smiled. "Let's find something to keep my hand flat. I'm not doing it on purpose."

Mellow led her away to the newly organized saddle bags.

"Astrid will get over it faster now she has a job," Luis

said. He handed Bebop's reins to Lena. "We could all do with a break from the bickering."

"You didn't say much about looking for people," Lena said.

"Don't know if it's a good idea or not, but this is the time, if you want to do it. We'll be in familiar territory soon."

"Do you think there are settlements?" she asked.

"Not from before. And no one could be in a camp during the plagues and survive. It took too long to pass to just wait it out, even though it seemed fast. People would have gone looking for help and brought it back with them."

"But now, it's a safe place," she said. "You can hunt and build a shelter. No need to worry about someone coming to look for you."

"Think about where they would come from," Luis said, waving his arm to encompass the whole area. "Northwest? That's unlikely given the story we heard in Crouch. East? There's a lot more hospitable places to stop. South? My first trip through there, people were already settled. Weather's better, farming is good."

"This trip's a bust," Lena said, feeling her dreams die. "We've covered a lot of the country without any success."

"You've met some good people. Me, Astrid, Beattie? You wouldn't know us if you stayed at the farm. Astrid would be dead by now if you hadn't taken her in."

"I didn't mean that," she said. "I'm scared. If everyone is happy to stay in their little world, no matter how bad, then there's no future for the country."

38

The next few days had gone smoothly. Even Astrid had calmed down about Beattie after they'd had a whispered conversation. Beattie's hand healed at a good pace, but she was still the first to fall asleep at night, and Lena suspected she napped in the saddle.

The scouting trip was helpful about side trails for short cuts. But no people. It was like humans had disappeared. The scouts found nothing to show any camp was recently occupied.

Now they were stopped in a place called Stanley Base-camp Lodge, the first sign of civilization since Crouch. This was the kind of place Lena meant when she said people should have migrated into the mountains at some point. Not some campsite with no amenities, but a resort. A place that would shelter people in comfort even without electricity or running water.

The lodge was huge, maybe a thousand rooms all facing the view over a canyon as far as Lena could see. The last person had tied the front door handles together with rope to keep out any animals. The parking lot filled the rest of the space at the top of a long rise. Half the spots were large enough to hold RVs. All the spots were empty, as if the place was waiting to hold its grand opening.

Someone had stocked the building before taking off. A note on the reception counter said to take what they needed. The plumbing was all gravity fed, so if there was water, it would work.

The note was signed with, *I'm headed back to civilization. This isn't a good place for a guy alone. Starting to go crazy.*

No one had come to the location by the look of the shelves in the storeroom. The fridges and freezers stunk because the generator failed. But cans and dried goods sat on shelves like it was the first day of the season.

"Check the rooms," Beattie said.

"There's Sterno," Luis said. "I'll see if I can get the wood stove heated."

Everyone else separated to explore the lodge. Beattie and Lena stood in the lobby, staring around.

"People knew the place was here. Hunters, hikers," Lena said. "Not everyone who used this place before fell to the plagues."

"Would you make the journey to see if it was still standing?" Beattie asked. "Through all that forest, without transportation?"

"I don't know. The parking lot is empty, and the road, too. If I knew about it and had gas? I'd have come pretty early. If I had to come some other way? No. Too risky. If this wasn't standing? Long way to the next place."

Beattie nodded. "It's still creepy, even knowing that," she said. "Like all the possibility is still holding its breath."

"We should stay a few days. Give you a chance to build stamina."

"And Astrid more time to baby me?" Beattie chuckled.

"I'm not sure that's a good idea. We can stay the night. It's going to be easy to secure the place, so we don't have to set people to watch during the night. The creepiness might be the only thing keeping us awake."

Luis joined them from outside. "Horses are in an old garage. I think I'll sleep with them tonight. Make sure we don't lose them to bears or cougars."

Splitting them up didn't feel right. Lena looked around the lobby. Too many places for a horse to get injured with the stairs and sunken lounge. And she didn't want to leave the place filled with dung and hay. "Will they be safe while we settle in here? Make food?"

"No. Unless we can find a way to build a door or drop the electric-powered one." Luis picked up his backpack. "Have someone bring me a meal."

"We need to talk tonight. All of us," Beattie said. "You need to be here for that. Let me come see what we can do to secure the newly assigned stables."

In the worst case, the entire group could eat in the stables and take turns watching. So much for a night off; Lena's thoughts swirled trying to solve the problems she saw all around her.

"The rooms were all sealed up," Astrid called from the top of the stairs. "A bit of dust, but ready for us to use."

"We'll leave them that way when we go," Lena called up.

"Where's Beattie?" Astrid asked, racing down the stairs.

Lena held up her hand to stop the girl's headlong rush. "With Luis. Trying to figure out how we can leave the horses in the garage. Come into the kitchen to see if Luis managed to light the stove."

In the kitchen, one of the wood burning stoves was warming. "It's going to take time to heat up enough."

"The rooms will be cold tonight," Astrid said.

"We've had worse." Lena started looking for pots and pans. "I wanted to talk to you."

"What have I done now?" Astrid started placing cans and bags of pasta on the stainless-steel prep table.

"Nothing," Lena said. "Just, if you were wounded, how would you want to be treated?"

"Beattie wants you to tell me to back off? Like I'll listen better if you tell me she's going to be okay?"

"No. This is coming from me. But fussing over her isn't helping. She's embarrassed, and I think she feels weak when you keep checking on her or telling us to make allowances. So, what's your answer?"

Astrid rolled her eyes, the grin on her face taking the sting out of the expression. "Fine. I'd be a giant pain because I'd be scared I was a burden."

"So? What are you going to do?" Lena pulled out a can opener.

"I guess I'll trust her to know she's going to be okay." Astrid tested the tap. Water ran brown, then clear. "How do we know this is good to drink and cook in?"

"Does it smell?" Lena joined her at the sink.

"No. But not all things that can kill us give warning."

"We'll boil it."

Luis and Beattie had managed to bring the garage door down and seal the place for the horses. "If we can't open it in the morning, we'll break it," Luis said.

They sat around the fire in the lounge and ate that night. The lobby warmed up, and the whole space felt cozy. Lena wanted to pretend they were on a weekend getaway. That the world outside was like before the plagues. But the emptiness surrounding them intruded, setting a chill along her shoulders, despite the fire.

"So where do we go next?" she asked.

39

"I'm coming around to the idea of going straight home," Scott said. "This emptiness is almost harder than the violence."

"There's a long way between here and there," Tik said. He pulled the map out and looked around for a place to spread it. "Kitchen."

They gathered around the prep table. Luis made coffee and added honey to each cup.

Tik put a ketchup package near their current location, and a sugar package near the farm. "No real straight run. We can go through the lower end of the same states we passed through last year so there's some new places to check out. No going looking for little settlements. Suburbs and cities will give us the best chance of making contact."

Lena traced the route. The rivers and mountains forced them to travel in a loop. Roads would be faster, but she remembered the feeling of being watched that drove them off the highway on the way down. Constantly questioning their route wasn't getting them anywhere. The closer they got to the farm, the fewer options the road provided. And the longer they traveled, the less she believed in the dream that drove her to come.

"It's going to take a couple of months," Scott said. "That's a long time without stopping somewhere. We have the time if we want to take it. Leaving early in the year made for a miserable start, but the weather will get better every day now."

"The route through Liberty isn't very far off that track," Astrid said. "We could come at it from a couple of different directions."

"If you are planning to get your revenge on Ivan, think again," Lena said. "He has too many friends, and we don't want to bring trouble with us when we leave."

"We'll see," she said. "We shouldn't avoid the place just because of him, either."

"Stopping and getting some supplies for the farm makes sense," Scott said. "We could go to Beta as well. See what they've invented in the last year."

"Liberty will have news, too," Tik said.

"I'll be healed enough in the next couple of days," Beattie said. "We can speed up and ride longer."

"We haven't slowed down much," Mellow said, "and you are being optimistic about your stamina."

"If you want to get news, we should visit Kiaiyo." Luis put his finger on the edge of the old Fort Peck reservation. "This time of year, he should be around the eastern edge, looking for game and training new horses."

"News is better than some kind of maybe alliance," Beattie said. "It will benefit home more to know what's heading toward us. We can train fighters for general defense, but knowing the threat gives us a good idea of what to prepare for, and what to scavenge."

She is talking about the farm as home, Lena thought. A

good sign that she'll fit in. "Are we adding to the threat by contacting people in other communities?"

"Everything is a threat if we don't seek out information," Scott said. "Are you saying we should build some walls around the farm and turn into one of these closed-off communities?"

"Not that extreme," Lena said. "It's hard not to get discouraged when we've only found bad people."

"You've seen some good communities," Astrid said. "Just because they are different from you doesn't mean they're completely bad. You talk about this Beta place. And Liberty, and when the bad leaders are replaced, Glass House and Pearl Two."

Her words surprised Lena. Had she been drawing too narrow a picture of a good community? "Yes, and Kiaiyo, and there were a few smaller places on the way out. But Virtue? Crouch? Nicolette's cult?"

"No one will want to be allies with them," Mellow said. "But they work for the people who live there. And none of them are planning a giant takeover that will threaten the farm."

"Don't give up," Beattie said. "Your idea is good. It's going to take a long time, that's all."

Time I don't have. Lena stopped the negative voice. She didn't have to be the one to unite the country. Getting the idea out there was the only way to spark the actions needed to make her dream a reality. The thoughts were nowhere near enough for her to feel positive, but enough to keep her hopeful.

"I've haven't been east much in the years I've been on the road," Luis said, changing the subject. "I'm happy to continue on with you. I'm thinking there's a lot of ground between the sugar pack and the Atlantic."

"Okay, home by fall then," Lena said. "See whatever we can on the way."

"One more day here?" Astrid said. "This is good terrain for target practice. None of us have used our bows much lately."

"Another day will give us time to figure out what we want to take," Mellow said. "Not all of it, and we'll leave the doors locked so the next person will have a chance."

"When you say take things, you mean the coffee?" Lena asked. "The honey?"

"We should fill our packs with things that are hard to get," Astrid said. "They'll buy us accommodation and food in Liberty. Maybe a wagon to carry more stuff to the farm."

Lena looked around the fully stocked cupboards. People had done without so much of this stuff for so long, would it be cruel to bring them back for a little while? For her, the answer was no. Having access to coffee, even stale beans, was worth it. "Anyone want to tackle the freezers?"

"Nothing in there will be edible," Luis said. "Or valuable."

"I meant to clean it out. Humans can't eat it, but there are animals who will. And the next people to come along won't have that stench in their nostrils." Lena figured she'd be catching the odor over the next few days until the fresh air scoured it from her nose.

"There's gloves and masks in the janitor's closet," Luis said. "Maybe we want to leave cleaning until our last day? There's probably a few things in the other store cupboards that should be tossed, anyway."

"Okay," Scott said. "It looks like our road heads through Bozeman and then Billings before heading to Nation One."

"And there's one more thing I found," Tik said. "If we're sure we don't need to set a watch on the horses or the hotel, we can use up some of these." He reached under the table and pulled up three bottles of wine.

"We can't risk them breaking in the bags if we take them," Luis said. "Three bottles won't get us drunk."

"Astrid and I will set up a few alarms," Beattie said. "Don't drink it all while we're gone."

40

Bozeman was inhabited. Lena felt a weight lift from her shoulders. Despite what they'd learned from people on the way, deep down she'd worried that some new plague was creeping across to take out the people she loved. She'd known it wasn't logical. No one would have lied about something like that, and very few people would have survived.

On the old welcome sign, someone had scrawled directions to where the people were set up. And they'd crossed out the population number a couple of times. The last time it had happened, whoever did it wrote. *Something around five thousand of us. I'm tired of counting and people come and go. So keep going, or come visit. It's up to you.*

"Can you imagine keeping a census?" Beattie asked. "Constantly learning how many people died."

"It's the first we've seen," Lena said. "The paint has faded, so who knows what we'll find."

"Do we all go?" Astrid asked. "I mean, the sign isn't threatening, exactly."

From their vantage point above the town, Lena checked

the road. "We have to go around it to continue to Billings. I say we all go."

No one argued, so they followed the directions into what had once been downtown. As they approached, a gang of children ran from the buildings and escorted them.

The kids told them to tie their horses to the railing and head inside. It wasn't quite an old west town, but someone had installed railings in spots along the streets. It reminded Lena of bicycle parking. A few horses were waiting for their riders, drinking from the trough placed below the railing.

The building was an old courtroom, and inside it was set up with a reception desk and waiting area. Someone was clearly making an effort to run the place like a town before.

The man sitting at the reception desk shooed the kids out and handed them a clipboard. "Just helps to have names," he said. "Mine is Joe."

Lena filled out the register for the whole group. Names, whether they planned to stay and how long. Area they came from. None of the questions were too personal. It seemed a good measure to take before letting anyone inside.

"You're planning to move on today?" Joe asked, reading the sheet of paper. "Why'd you come in?"

"It's been a long time since we've come across a community," Scott said. "I guess curiosity more than anything."

"The mayor will be out in a minute. You want to grab a meal, or supplies, we work on trade here."

"Thanks, we'll just wait," Lena said.

They settled on the wooden benches lining the walls in the waiting area. "Brian would have loved this," Mellow said. "Official, and showing that someone is in charge. Maybe he's set this kind of thing up where they settled."

"I think it's easier here than in most places," Lena said. "The cities and towns around here existed in the old west times. They'll have a lot of history getting along without modern conveniences. And if there are still five thousand or so residents, that's a lot of people to share the work."

"What if this is where the people in the north came to?" Astrid asked. "Some of them must have gotten past Crouch."

Lena didn't answer because the double doors behind them opened, and the end of a conversation drifted to their position.

"I'm sure you'll figure something out, sheriff. A balance between keeping the peace and letting the kids burn off some of that excess energy." The speaker was a woman, and she followed the sheriff out. In her fifties and dressed like she was going to brunch with her country club girl-friends.

She nodded to Joe, who came up and told her about the visitors waiting.

The sheriff, a bandy-legged man wearing jeans and a button-down shirt with a badge embroidered on the left chest nodded to Lena and then stuck his cowboy hat on before pushing the door open.

"Come on in," the mayor said. "Joe, bring in some water. These people look thirsty."

Joe nodded and left them with the mayor.

Lena introduced her whole group. The mayor, Wilda Keene, shook hands all around and then asked what she could do for them.

"I guess we were just hoping there were people here," Scott said. "We've come from the coast and a lot of abandoned settlements. Whole cities. How did you manage to keep this setup?"

Joe walked in with a tray of glasses filled with water and a plate of sandwiches. Bread seemed to be the one constant pantry item. Grinding flour wasn't so high tech. Growing wheat for a few people wasn't exactly easy, but it wasn't impossible.

"We just pulled together from the beginning. I got elected mayor when the old one succumbed to the plague. We all agreed the place needed rules. We already supplied most of our food locally. Kind of miss TV, but we have less time to just sit and watch anyway. People. I guess that's my answer. We don't have a lot of stupid rules. Everyone got a say in the setup. We do what we have to. No one here is willing to take shit from anyone. We had enough of that nonsense before most of the community died out."

The speech was well practiced. Like it was a message for anyone looking to settle; fit in or move along.

"What about the rest of the country?" Astrid asked, preempting Lena's question. "I mean, it's great that you're all safe, but there's a lot bad out there. It will come here eventually."

"The rest of the country is capable of taking care of itself," Wilda said. "We've dealt with trouble before and we'll deal with it again. Joining up to some kind of country brings rules we don't get a say in. And plenty of greedy people find a way to use the rules to take what they think should be theirs."

That was the nicest way they'd been told no during the whole trip.

"I guess we should head out," Lena said. She thought back to the conversation at the lodge. Bozeman was another community on the list of ones that were healthy but not interested. "Thanks for the hospitality."

"I'd appreciate it if you don't let people know about us," Wilda said. "We take in anyone who finds us if they seem decent. We don't need a bunch of assholes coming to steal from us because they think we're weak."

. . .

THE LAST PLACE they'd chosen to visit was very different from Bozeman. From their stop on the road above the city, they could see Billings was surrounded by makeshift fences and patrolled by men on horseback dressed in knight costumes and carrying swords.

"It could be for show," Tik said. "It's not armor. From here, I think it's tinfoil-covered cardboard."

Lena lifted her own binoculars. "Those are real swords."

"The guards are only on the main entrance," Beattie said. "We should move on."

"You think Bozeman knows about this?" Scott asked.

"Yes," Luis said. "All that talk about assholes trying to take their stuff. We're looking at the assholes."

"We should move on to Liberty," Astrid said. "These guys might just be unhinged, but I'm guessing they want to use those blades."

"Your decision," Scott said.

Lena put her binoculars into their case and sighed. For every strong community, how many were like this? Primed for a fight that wasn't coming.

"Nation One and then Liberty," she said. "Those guards will see us pass on the road, so be ready if they move toward us."

41

I t was eerie the way Kiaiyo seemed to always be where they wanted him. This was a different mesa than the one they'd been at before. But it only took a couple of hours for the leader of Nation One to appear from below. Still dressed in his faded cowboy gear. A new scar on his cheek. The same battered hat on his head.

"You've seen some things," Kiaiyo said. "Are you visiting or reporting?"

"We can stick around a couple of days if you need something," Luis said. "We're on our way past. Thought you might want to know what things are like west of here. What we found, what we didn't."

Kiaiyo sat and took the tea Mellow offered. "I have time to talk around the fire and get your news. The tribe is busy with the births. Foals are dropping every day now. Visitors disturb the mares. I also have events to share as payment for your tale."

"What do you do with the extra horses?" Astrid asked.

"What makes you think we have extra?" Kiaiyo smiled as he spoke.

"Math."

"I see your wild warrior has matured a little," he said to Lena. "Still wild, but your ways are different."

"Training helped," Lena said. "Beattie joined us from a military camp. Add to that what we've experienced in the last few months, and you get instant growing up."

"Life makes us what we need to be. Tell me your story first," Kiaiyo said. "Mine will not take long."

Luis shared their experiences in chronological order, starting with the cult and Fort Revelation, both seemed benign in comparison to the more recent communities. He spent more time explaining what happened in Pearl Two, ending with Bozeman.

"Billings is populated," he said. "Not with people we want to know. And they didn't look like they ventured out much."

Kiaiyo sat through the recitation, sipping his tea and nodding to show he was listening. "Most are too far to worry me," he said. "The monks, maybe. Lots of religions popping up. None of them have been beneficial to my people from the first time they stepped foot on this land."

"Or ours since the plagues," Lena said. "Nowadays, they all seem to be the apocalyptic version."

"We will watch for them," Kiaiyo said. "Sounds like the ones you ran into won't know how to fight Indian style."

Lena shifted on the flat rock. She'd been hoping Kiaiyo would have a different take on the events. He was more interested in keeping people out than he'd been before, and he'd been less than welcoming the last time they came.

His words seemed to burn the last of her vision of a united country from her heart. It was good they were going home; she would feel like she had value there. Out here, the survivors were still raw from the grief of losing so many people and a whole way of life. It was too soon. No matter what her job should be in the process of creating a new nation, she'd done enough. Maintaining a strong local bond was probably all she would manage. Maybe her passion for the vision kept waning because her part was over.

"You want some more tea?" Beattie asked. "Or we can get a meal going."

"I am not thirsty or hungry. You didn't see more of my people?"

"Like Nation One?" Scott asked. "No. As part of other places? Hard to tell."

"Pity. I may send scouts to seek out my own allies."

"You said you have news for us," Tik said. "Good or bad?"

"We will not know that until much later," Kiaiyo said. "For now, it has the feel of something good for us. Perhaps I am missing some signs of repercussions since we stay inside our borders."

Lena didn't want to interrupt Kiaiyo. The man had an air of gravitas she suspected was deliberate with strangers. His humor came out too frequently to make her believe he was naturally so serious. But it was getting late. They would be fine camped on the high ground, but he would have to navigate the narrow path down to the bottom when he left.

"A new threat?" she asked to gently prompt him.

"No, but with your news, I think we have underestimated an old one." He put his mug on the ground. "The men who stole Astrid. They didn't leave us alone after the warning we gave. We were forced to hunt them."

"You killed them all?" Astrid asked, sounding disappointed that she'd missed the opportunity.

"We cut off the head," Kiaiyo said. "At least we thought so, but perhaps this is similar to the ancient Hydra. I think my idea of scouting the area must be put into action. If this gang is the same as that on the coast, they will not give up. They may be gathering strength as we sit here."

The idea gave Lena the chills. "Maybe the people we rescued are keeping them busy. And we didn't have any idea they were operating around home. So, they aren't too far spread."

"You are in old Canada," Kiaiyo said. "That is where the stolen are being taken."

"I did think of that," she said, "but our home is very close to where the old border ran. Maybe we've been lucky, maybe not. Things will have changed since we left."

"I hope it's not luck," Astrid said. "It can turn bad fast."

"We need to send someone to check on the city people we settled west," Lena said. "If the gangs are run from those settlements, they might not be safe."

"Something to worry about when we get home," Scott said. "We can't detour that far north. Winter will trap us."

Kiaiyo stood. "I am sorry to have raised such fears. I wish you good luck on your travels. Where will you stop next?"

"Liberty," Lena said. "Do some trading before we start the long ride."

"Things have changed there," he said. "We do not trade with the market anymore, but rumors reach us. Be careful."

The next morning, they headed toward Liberty. In no rush, they took the time to rest along the way. The nagging question of what Kiaiyo meant was the topic of every nighttime discussion.

"If something is wrong there, we don't want to arrive exhausted," Beattie said. "And we're setting camp outside before we commit."

"If we do that, someone will have to stay with the horses and supplies," Lena said. "We get close enough to assess the situation. If it's still a market, there's not much that can go wrong. If not, we head on to our next stop."

The easiest route home went past Liberty, so there was no point in trying to avoid it completely. Lena counted on the value of their trade goods to pay their way. Gathering a few new items to take home would only take a day or two. By the time they left Liberty, they should know what Kiaiyo meant with his comment.

"Is our next stop home?" Astrid asked. "Like, we'll go straight to the farm? Or do me and Beattie get to see other places?"

"The only other place worth checking is Beta," Scott said. "I bet Da Vinci would love to hear our adventures."

Lena thought about the months ahead of them, even if they avoided the towns they'd passed last year. The highway wouldn't be much better. Too many places to get trapped. If she remembered correctly, most of them took a big sidetrack or loop to avoid as many small communities as possible, leaving them with long sidetracks from one off ramp to the next on ramp.

On the way out, they'd stepped off the major routes because those tended to move directly from city to city, rather than the smaller towns. Even then, big cities were dangerous. And Tik was anxious enough traveling in the open to infect the others with a feeling of being watched.

"I don't think we should plan that far ahead," she said. "Let's see what's going on in Liberty first."

"Fair enough," Luis said. "I wasn't looking forward to months of just traveling, anyway."

All Lena wanted was to avoid everyone and get home. Every stop increased her fears that something had changed at the farm, something for the worse. Something she would be too late to stop.

"Are there any cities near the farm?" Beattie asked.

"None close," Scott said. "When we settled Poorjohn's people, we checked the area pretty well. Winnipeg was shut down to visitors, and that's the biggest city near us. It was at least a month's travel, if you moved fast."

"So, maybe the gang isn't there because the distances are too long to drag captives to their headquarters?" Lena's worry eased a little. If there was a believable reason the area around the farm was safe, she might be able to relax.

"Makes sense. You think we should head back through the closest bigger places?" Tik asked. "See if our neighborhood is getting dangerous? Or if there are signs of a new route west?"

"It wouldn't hurt," Beattie said. "Even if no one is planning an attack, getting some perspective would help. I thought it was just me. The wound and feeling weak, but I've been watching us and we're all feeling hopeless, right?"

That was exactly the emotion Lena felt. Not depression, but hopelessness, and a touch disappointed that people were so awful.

"So, if we find thriving communities, we'll be happier?" Mellow asked. "And if we find danger, we can be prepared."

"Something like that," Beattie said.

"It wasn't the danger that got us down," Lena said. "I mean, it was a bit, but all those empty places. I can't shake the feeling something is coming that will leave everywhere empty. No matter if you live in Pearl Two or Bozeman, no one is safe."

"We missed a lot of that," Astrid said. "And even though I wasn't welcome in Fort Revelation, I was relieved it hadn't changed. I guess I don't like the not knowing."

Talking about the possibilities helped, Lena thought. "I guess if something that bad is on its way, we can't do anything about it. Maybe talking through a plan will help bring some hope, and the future will look less bleak."

"No decisions," Luis said. "We need to see Liberty before we choose any plan. But coming up with ideas can't hurt, right?"

Lena wondered again if Luis planned to join them at the farm. He seemed to identify himself more as one of them as time passed. The request would have to come from him. She was certain the whole family would welcome him. If he wasn't planning on settling anywhere, turning them down might cause him to leave them to avoid dealing with any uncomfortable feelings.

And he'd lost his kids to the plague. Perhaps he wasn't ready to settle down in a place with other kids.

"Okay," she said. "We should also figure out what we're willing to trade at the market, and what we want to buy. Learn what we can about the changes. I don't want to hang around long." Mostly because she wasn't sure any of them could control Astrid if she met up with — or sought out — Ivan.

43

From the outside, Liberty looked the same as when they'd left it almost a year ago. People came and went without any indication of distress or coercion. The metal walls still stood strong. At first glance, the entrance looked much smaller. Lena looked more carefully and saw the whole thing was reconfigured. Two gates. The one for people riding or leading horses was open and tended by a guard. The other, wide enough for wagons, was shut.

From their position near a copse of trees, they were all able to see the activity. Liberty wasn't like the other places they'd observed. No high point to watch from a safe distance, and no other option but to ride past the gates if they decided to move on. Here, they were in plain view, but no one seemed to pay any attention.

"I say a couple of us go in and register the group," Mellow said. "Everyone else and our horses stay here. We'll signal for you to come in if it seems safe."

"And if it isn't?" Tik asked. "What do we do? Come on a rescue mission?"

"Not right away," Beattie said. "If there's a problem, we'll just get caught up in it. We leave. Go far enough that the people inside think we've abandoned whoever is inside. Then we come back on a rescue mission. Probably through that back gate."

If it still exists, Lena thought. "Should we just go on?" she asked. "What do they have that we really need?"

"No," Scott said. "We don't just go past. It's too far for us to come back if we need something. It looks like nothing has changed. Beattie's plan is right. We just need to figure out who goes in."

"I'll go," Luis said. "If my buddies are still in residence, I can get the real story. And I'm not a threat."

"We need Beattie and Astrid for the rescue mission," Lena said. "That leaves me, Scott, Mellow, or Tik to go with Luis. Any reason one or the other should go? Or does anyone want to stay out here?"

"You don't need a fighter to go in," Mellow said. "No need to antagonize anyone in there. I want to see for myself."

"No, just two of us. I'll come with you, Luis," Lena said. "If there's a problem and we're taken, they don't have the key people."

"What do you mean?" Scott asked. "You and Luis are important."

"Not for this. Luis is right; his friends will be the best source of information. I'm the weakest fighter. I know I can probably outfight most of the people inside those walls, but you are all far better at it than me. And Mellow is our doctor. I don't want her captured."

She didn't voice the main reason because it wasn't the strongest argument. If she had to wait outside, she'd wear herself out with worry and still want firsthand information.

"I'm not going to argue," Scott said. "Just be careful and fast. How long do you think we should wait?"

"Half an hour," Luis said. "It might take a while to get through the process if it's toughened up. I don't like it that Kiaiyo didn't give us details. The changes could be simple, like higher security or just something that annoys him. Or... well, we all have our own worst case scenario, right?"

Lena handed Bebop's reins to Mellow and checked her hidden knives were secure. "Let's go."

"You were here before," the woman at the gate said. "Where's the rest of your group?"

"You remember us?" Lena wasn't sure how to feel about that.

"I remember Luis came through with a group last year. Unusual for him. You need work?"

"We'll trade this time," Luis said. "Couple of days."

"Just the two of you?" the woman asked.

"Maybe," Lena said. "How much will we be shelling out for food and lodging?"

"It's a bit chaotic these days," the woman said. "We got busier than we expected. You can pitch a camp of your own around the stables. A few coins worth of trade charged by the space, not the people."

"We'll do that," Lena said. Leaving someone at the camp inside to watch the horses and supplies was much easier than doing it outside. With everyone together, no one was left to imagine disasters. And if Liberty was chaotic, they couldn't rely on whatever security the market offered.

"If the rest of your group is coming in, go get them now," the woman said. "Easier to check everyone in at once."

"Are my buddies here?" Luis asked.

"Those reprobates?" The woman laughed. "A couple in the usual place and up to the usual antics."

Luis headed off to bring the remaining people in. "Any new rules?" Lena asked.

"Other than the curfew? No. The challenge is enforcing the old ones. Too many people, not enough guards. The gate closes at sundown and doesn't open until sunrise. What you do inside during the shutdown is up to you."

Lena started filling out the paperwork while she waited for Luis to organize the rest of the party. The woman hadn't lied. The same rules were listed, but someone had increased the prices of everything. Setting up their camp was first on the list, getting their trade items converted to coin chits was second. Third might just be wandering around, scoping out the market to see if they could find the trouble Kiaiyo mentioned. And assess what they might be able to afford.

"We'll get through the trading tomorrow," Lena said. "Leave at first light on the next day."

"Whatever works for you, and you have the credit to pay for." The woman collected everyone's sign-in sheets and glanced over the contents. "You keep your weapons sheathed or pay for a locker. You get into a fight, you go to a cell. That's one rule we enforce no matter how busy."

44

A t their assigned plot, Luis dropped his backpack, unloaded Angel's bags, and led the horses to the stables. Four other camps were set up, all with a single guard watching. None of them in the uniform of Liberty's patrol.

"Sort out the trade packs," Lena said to Tik. "We need to find a place where we can talk. This is too public."

He placed the backpacks in a circle where people would sleep. "We'll get this set up, go chat with the guards and get an idea of what we're dealing with. I don't know if we want to stay two nights. I got a bad feeling we're missing something big."

Lena had the same feeling. Their route from the gate to the camp took a wide circle around the market. At the edges it looked fine, the same stalls with clothes, equipment and food. The noises coming from farther in were very different from last year. Not the chatter of deals and gossip, but noisier, like there was a fight going on, or some kind of violent contest people were betting on. None of that had been in evidence before.

She walked over to the closest guard. A man huddled over a small fire, a mug of tea cradled in his hands, the stink of dope emanating from his clothes.

"Hi," she said. "We're setting up for a few days."

"Keep to yourself," the man said. "Leave us alone."

"Ignore him," a woman called from the next camp. She looked like she was in her forties, a bit older than Lena, some Asian heritage with a thick braid hanging down to her waist, sliver strands running through black. "I'm Anne, if you want to chat."

Lena walked over and introduced herself. "We're just wondering how much of a security presence we need to have. Looks like one person is enough."

"Don't pay for the hired guards," Anne said. "He's one of them. Falls asleep half the time, stoned most of the rest. Where are you from?"

"Back east," Lena said. Friendliness didn't mean harmless. "You?"

"Same, place called Beta."

"How long ago did you leave?" She didn't remember meeting this woman during her stay.

"A few months. Looking for new markets. You heading that way?"

Lena glanced over to where their camp was taking shape. No fire yet, but the makings were stacked nearby. "Not sure yet," she said. "We need to do a bit of trading."

"Good luck. I'll be heading out soon. A few of my agreements have to be finalized."

IT TOOK a bit more haggling than Lena anticipated to get their coin chits. The attitude of the boy in the booth was more aggressive than before, and Lena didn't see many familiar faces. She had no idea if that was unusual, or if it was proof of something wrong. Like she was collecting all the little indicators that would, in hindsight, add up to a big, blinking warning sign. Knowing she had to accept it was one thing, feeling good about it was another.

Luis had gone in search of his friends, Beattie was watching their camp, and the others were waiting for her outside the assessor's office.

"You want me to deduct your horse and camp costs or pay direct?" the man she'd negotiated with asked, bringing her attention back to the task.

"Is there a benefit?" Paying now would save her the time of locating the people who'd take her daily chits. And doing so would also take away any uncertainty about how much they could spend.

"Pay me and you get a discount. If you leave early, you don't get a refund. Pay them, you just pay for what you use."

The discount was enough to make prepaying a good deal. If they had to leave early, it meant things had gone completely sideways, and lost coin wouldn't even be on the bottom of her list of worries.

Outside, she handed each person their share of the chits. "You all know what you're responsible for," she said. "We should just see what's available today and talk about it tonight."

"We all need to be involved in the conversation," Astrid said. "That means we hire someone to watch our stuff, or we talk at the camp. What's better?"

Neither, Lena thought. "I don't want to pay money to someone just to sit there like the next camp over. We'll talk there, just keep it quiet. No talk about where we're headed," she said.

"I'm going with Astrid," Tik said. "We'll head over to the

weapons stalls. We don't need anything, but if there's trouble, it will be around those vendors."

"Stay away from Ivan," Lena said, "if he's still here."

"I will," Astrid said. "I'm smarter than I was before. If I decide to take him on, it'll be when we're leaving and with Beattie at my side."

Being smarter would mean she'd just avoid the man altogether, Lena thought. "Let's meet back at camp by five?" She checked her watch. "We'll bring a meal, no point in using up our travel supplies. Mellow and Scott, do you have any specific places you want to check out?"

"I'm going to check the clinic," Mellow said. "It wasn't that busy when we were here. Maybe I can figure out what's going on by seeing who's in for treatment."

She was alone with Scott for the first time in months. Lena looped her arm through his. "Let's see what we can find for the farm."

"Or we can enjoy some alone time," he whispered, leaning in to plant a kiss on her cheek. "One good thing about getting home is we'll have time to ourselves again."

"I miss it," she said. "Pearl Two was almost like home but you were so exhausted by working in the foundry, you fell asleep as soon as you got into bed, most times."

As they strolled through the market, Lena noticed some of their trade items were already laid on the food stalls. Not a surprise, the spices were rare these days. She'd kept back a container of each for the farm. If they really needed to raise more coins, she'd trade, but everyone agreed their home should benefit from their travels, too.

"It's quieter," Scott said.

"Yes, no sound of fighting. Or whatever that was before."

"Not fighting," Scott said. "A fight. Look over there."

In the center of the market, a space had been cleared for

a new platform. Ropes around the edges and a canvas floor declared its purpose. An old-fashioned boxing ring. The bleachers set around three edges of the square were on wheels. Between fights, the space would be clear.

"I don't like that," Lena said. "It opens the door to criminal activity. Wasn't gambling prohibited? Or kept to friendly card games, something like that?"

"And what happened to 'you start a fight and you go to jail'? No way the violence is contained by the ropes." Scott looked around. "Is there anything else different?"

"We can't just ask," Lena said. "Look at how people are pretending this isn't here." Customers continued to barter while studiously not paying attention to the arena.

"Luis' friends will tell him, but look around. Do you see anything other than the fighting ring that raises concerns?"

The ground of the fight ring was sand. Someone had raked it over since the fight they'd heard, but dark blotches still showed in places. Not water, blood.

"It's not boxing," she said.

"Bare fists," a woman said. "You shouldn't stand here too long. Gets noticed, you might find yourself inside the ropes."

Lena recognized her. She'd been in charge of the accommodations last year. Now she was wearing worn clothes that were covered in a fine dust. "It's a surprise," she said. "What happened? You were collecting rents last time."

"Yeah, well, now I'm sweeping up. Do what you're told or get out. I don't have skills to survive on the road."

"Why did things change?" Scott asked.

"Mind your business and you won't need to know," the woman said as she walked away.

"It feels like the plague was just the first try at killing everyone off," Lena said. "Human nature is taking care of the rest."

"There are still good people," Scott said. "Most of them seem to live around us, but not everyone is going bad. There could be a reason, and it might be temporary. Without real news, we shouldn't make decisions."

"Fine, let's see how much our list is going to cost us. I want us out of here before we're trapped."

45

A t the camp, Beattie and Anne were chatting when Lena arrived with Scott.

"We can use the tables over there," Beattie said, pointing to a cluster of picnic benches a little distance away from the fires. "I can keep an eye on the camp from there. No one is around, so if we don't linger, we'll have all the privacy we need."

The wood on the table had seen better days. Left in the sun to dry out and split, it needed to be covered unless they were willing to risk splinters. It wouldn't have taken much to maintain it, but no one had bothered.

Lena tossed one of the sleeping bags on top as a table-cloth and then set up the meal of sandwiches and sweet buns she'd brought. Scott added jugs of milk. Somewhere in the last months, Liberty had acquired cows and chickens. She hoped it wasn't because they'd stolen the livestock off some innocent family.

Mellow joined them a few minutes later. Tik and Astrid took seats on the bench. Luis trailed in after them. No one looked happy, but she didn't notice any fear, either. Perhaps the news wasn't as bad as she expected.

Anne had walked away from her camp when Beattie joined Lena. A man sat there now, stirring the fire to life. He wasn't one of the paid guards because he was alert to anyone approaching without being obvious.

Whoever set up the picnic tables had been careful to place them away from curious ears.

"Let's talk fast," Astrid said, "before anyone else comes to use the tables."

"Does anyone think we should get out now?" Tik asked. "We can eat and be gone in a few minutes. Reports can wait."

"It's different," Mellow said, "but not enough to make me want to run."

"The market is still operating," Scott said. "I think we stick to our plan and trade. We should be able to get most of what we wanted, even though the prices have gone up."

"Luis, you probably have the closest to the truth from your friends," Lena said. "You go first."

"I need to get some context to make sense of it," Luis said. "I didn't exactly get real details. Mostly bitching about the changes."

Scott gave a brief account of what he and Lena observed. "It seems rougher. Unless people are being forced to fight for some reason, I think it's probably just a new moneymaker."

"The clinic is the same people," Mellow said. "More injuries, but if people are fighting, then that makes sense. I'm not sure the doctor and nurses were free to talk. Nothing overt, just a feeling they wanted me to stop asking questions."

"The weapons stalls are full," Tik said. "Lots of trade going on. Some new faces there."

"That guy who wouldn't sell me nunchucks is gone," Astrid said. "Maybe he didn't like the new merchandise. We saw more than just knives and bows. Handcuffs, those plastic ones that zip closed. A few shackles."

"I don't like that," Lena said. "Did you see who was buying?"

"They weren't wearing signs," Tik said. "Might be police from towns around. Might be the gang members. Kiaiyo got rid of a lot, but he said it wasn't enough."

"They can't take us," Astrid said. "We're aware of them. Last time I wasn't trained, and I got taken by surprise."

"That woman," Beattie said, nodding toward Anne's camp. "We got talking. She says people disappear from here. But she thinks it's just mostly runaways. She didn't mention fighting. If we hang around, we need to be careful not to get drawn into anything."

Luis took one of the sweet buns and placed it on the table in front of him. He waited until they were all looking at him before speaking.

"I guess I've heard enough to know my buddies didn't exaggerate that much. There's been a change in leadership. Ivan is in charge, but he does it from behind a new council — all his buddies. The sports, as he put it, started the day after he took the reins. The old council is working the worst jobs and can't leave. If they try, he'll drag them back and stick them in the ring. No one likes it, but most people just keep out of trouble."

"Most people?" Astrid asked. "That means someone is fighting back?"

"Just talk," Luis said. "You stay out of it. We're stuck here until sunrise. I say we trade fast and get out."

"So, the guys buying from the weapons stalls? Gang members? The restraints are for people they kidnap?" Astrid asked, her voice hissing with anger. "And we're okay with that?"

Beattie put her hand on the girl's arm. "We can't do anything about it. This isn't like Glass House, no one is asking for our help."

"Yeah, and I'm the only one who they'll take, right?" Astrid asked. "They like their victims young."

"And compliant," Lena said. "You said yourself that you're too well trained now for them to take you."

"Not if they drug me or knock me out," Astrid said. "But what about the kids here? Are we just leaving them to be stolen?"

"We don't know enough," Beattie said. "Who do we go after? What kind of weapons, how many of them? We'd end up dead, and some of the people who die with us are going to be innocent."

Astrid stood and pushed her half-eaten sandwich to the center of the table. "I can't sit here talking. I'll be back by the last watch. Some of the stalls are still open. Shopping will give me something to do."

She stormed away before anyone could react. Her rage was understandable, but Lena agreed with Beattie. Even with an army of warriors, Kiaiyo hadn't eradicated the gang. How were they supposed to make a difference?

At least they'd kept their voices low. The people around them didn't know anything more than a teenager had stomped out. Not a rare occurrence. The words she'd flung at them about being okay with what was happening stung. Lena wasn't like other leaders. She wasn't just looking after her own people. The odds of failure were simply too high.

46

L ena was awake when Astrid returned for her shift to watch the camp. The girl bought almost half of their wish list and packed the bags by firelight.

The waking camp was quiet the next morning. As though people believed making noise would bring the wrong kind of attention. Lena poked the fire and started the water for oatmeal. They'd use their own food and save the chits for the merchant stalls. Now that she was aware of the change in leadership, she interpreted every look and whisper as a threat. Sleeping in those conditions wasn't an option.

"We need to be out of here fast," she whispered to Astrid.

"The horses and supplies should go now," Astrid said. "We can carry everything left on the list if we need to. There are a few horses for sale, but we don't have enough chits."

If they were about to leave, why would splitting the group be worthwhile? Lena would put money on Astrid being up to something. "We shop as soon as the stalls open and we're gone, Astrid."

"I met some people last night," Astrid whispered. "Resistance. Get the camp to safety, Mellow is not a good fighter. She can take care of that while we..." she trailed off.

"What?" Lena asked. "You said you'd stay out of it. Did you do something to involve us? Because you want to get Ivan?"

"No, you told me not to get involved. I never agreed."

Beattie joined them at the fire. "That's a fine line, Astrid. We can't solve all the problems we encounter on the way home. Every time we fight, we leave enemies who might come for revenge."

Astrid blew out a frustrated breath. "I was careful."

"How do you know that?" Lena asked. "This could be a trap."

Beattie took the boiling pot off the heat and added the ingredients for breakfast. "No point in arguing about something that's done. So, what was your plan?"

Astrid seemed oblivious to Beattie's fury. Lena was sure that behind the woman's anger was fear. Astrid's rashness was going to turn deadly at some point. Perhaps being at the farm would calm her enough to survive her thirst for vengeance. There was no doubt that getting back at Ivan was driving the girl. Her sense of justice, too, but without the vengeance to stoke the flames, would she be defying Beattie?

"I want you to talk to the people I met last night," Astrid said. "Not all of us, just you, Lena, and Beattie. If I'm wrong, we can go. If I'm right, there's going to be a blowout soon. Like, in the next couple of days, soon."

"And you want us to fight along with them?" Lena asked. The sound of the others rising covered their conversation. Scott took over the breakfast prep, Luis headed to the stable, and Tik sat next to Mellow, pretending to chat. They were leaving the decision to the three of them.

Lena glanced at the other camps. No one was paying them any mind. The hired guard was back in place, waiting for the two merchants to leave before he started his shift. Anne was back at the fire, not paying attention. Or was she too casual? Lena pushed the thought aside. Sure, paranoia was an asset if they were really facing a rebellion, but the woman hadn't done anything to deserve her suspicion.

"Should we send Mellow out?" Lena asked Beattie.

"Yes, but not so openly. We should all go with the camp. Let the leaders think we're on our way out. We three come back in to do our final shopping."

"We'll meet these people you found," Lena said to Astrid. "Regardless of what's about to happen, we need information. Astrid, you can't make any promises about what we'll do from now on."

"I can do what I want."

The teenage attitude was back. Lena's experience as a teacher told her it would fade over time and often didn't have anything to do with external triggers. In the times before teenagers could be indulged. If Astrid didn't get control of herself, there would be a lot more blood in her future.

"If you can't work for the benefit of the whole group, we'll leave you here," Beattie said. "Getting on the superhero bandwagon is fine when it's you and me. We aren't alone any longer."

Astrid blanched at the idea Beattie would leave without her. Lena didn't believe it for a second, but that didn't matter if the girl stopped stepping over the line and putting everyone at risk.

She stood and spoke loud enough for their neighbors to

hear, "Let's pack up. We don't have much more to buy, so we should move out now. I don't want to get stuck by the curfew."

WHEN MELLOW WAS SETTLED about a mile away, the rest of the group returned to Liberty. "Do we all go to the meeting?" Scott asked on the walk back. "I know, Astrid, she's trying to control the uncontrollable. You don't want us to join you, but getting separated isn't smart."

"Buy the stuff on the list," Beattie said. "One of you take it to Mellow. That way, everything is outside. We'll go to the meeting as planned. We can regroup in, what, two hours? At the tavern near the center of the market?"

"Okay, be careful," Scott said quietly. Then, raising his voice as they walked through the gate, "Whoever gets to the tavern first buys the first round."

Astrid led Lena and Beattie a twisted route through the stalls to a small hotel that backed up against the wall. Or more correctly, the wall was built to block off any back entrance. Liberty had a handful of hotels all shoved away from the main action, all designed to funnel people through one door.

"We aren't being followed," Beattie said. "Is this the place, or are we moving again?"

"Here," Astrid said. "Just stick close. I didn't tell them you were both coming."

She led them to the basement of the hotel, sliding through a hidden door after looking around the lobby. It was darker in the basement, but three lanterns sat at the far end of the corridor. Rooms opened off the hall and as they passed, Lena peeked inside one. Storage, old boxes of documents as far as she could see.

Astrid knocked on the last door to the right, a complicated sequence that screamed 'something here is secret' to anyone who might overhear.

The door opened and a man peeked out. The sight of him gave the whole story an air of reality.

This was the merchant who refused to sell Astrid weapons she couldn't handle. He'd pointed Lena in the direction of Ivan and warned her of the dangers. There was no way he would be involved with whatever Ivan was doing to Liberty now.

47

The merchant beckoned them inside with a stare at Astrid. "I said only Lena."

"Well, you got a bonus. Where's everyone?"

The room was empty, but there were clear signs that several people spent a great deal of time here. A cleared space where they could draw out battle plans. A pile of drop sheets in the corner that, by the marks in the dust, looked like they'd been dragged around a few times. A camp stove with kettle, cups, and tea leaves tucked beside the cover so they could be hidden with little effort. Nothing a casual glance would give away. But if you knew an uprising was coming, the signs were there.

The man put a rolled-up tarp at the bottom of the door to muffle their whispers.

"How did you find Astrid?" Beattie asked before he could start talking.

"I saw her in the afternoon," the man said. "I'm Colin, by the way."

"How did you get her down here?" Lena asked.

"Told her I could help her with Ivan," Colin said. "I

know it was risky, but the girl has reason to want him punished."

"Not just risky, manipulative." Beattie sent a glare at Astrid.

"If we do this right, she'll get him."

Colin didn't have any remorse for his actions. Lena couldn't blame him, but he should have thought through the ramifications first.

"Who else is involved?" Lena asked. "And what exactly have you got planned?"

"I told you," Astrid said, "getting Liberty back from the assholes who run it now."

"How did that happen?" Beattie asked. "I've heard Astrid's story. The kidnapping aside, Liberty sounded pretty stable."

"The Indians," Colin said. "I don't blame them. They killed a lot of Ivan's people. I guess it created a vacuum. Ivan acted fast and made sure people learned right away what opposition meant."

"What does it mean to have him in charge?" Lena asked. "From the outside, Liberty is a bit rougher than before, but the market still runs. We did our business without problems. Other than that fighting ring, I don't see anything bad enough for you to risk people dying."

"The market is where Ivan recruits. We figure he reports up to the guys at the top of the gang. Made a deal. He sends them a cut of the trades and a few captives each month, they let him run the place. You can't see the worst of it. People disappearing. Anyone stupid enough to speak up goes in the ring against one of his fighters."

"How long?" Lena hadn't thought to ask Kiaiyo for the timing, and she wasn't sure he would have answered, anyway.

"Not long after you left. The market is quiet in the winter. Some people come, but mostly it's just the residents. We had no way to call for help, and by the time business picked up, Ivan had us under control. Or we let him think that." Colin offered them tea. No one accepted. "You want to know why we're acting now, right? That's the next question I'd be asking."

Beattie nodded at him.

"It takes a while to set up a revolt if you aren't a blood-thirsty asshole. We want Liberty back, and we want people to come and trade. Can't do that if customers are scared of slaughter. So, we made our plans, stocked up on what we needed, kept our eyes open. Now is because we're ready and if we wait, Ivan will have too tight a hold."

"Won't the people he deals with react?" Beattie asked. "They'll lose the income and the people."

Colin grinned. "Well, that's a bit of news Astrid supplied. Seems Kiaiyo isn't the only one fighting back. She says the coast is in revolt. They'll be pretty busy defending the entire business."

"In revolt is a bit of an exaggeration," Lena said, "but it's good logic."

"And this time, you can set up defenses so they can't operate here," Astrid said.

"We can, and I'm already trying to figure out how to get Kiaiyo to work with us on that. But as long as people don't give a shit about their neighbors, we're weak. So, getting back to what we had before is the first priority," Colin said. "Are you going to help?"

Was that the way to unite communities? Let them do it locally, then tie cluster to cluster when people had a chance to see the benefit? Lena's dream wouldn't let go. One minute, she was convinced they were better off hunkering down at the farm, and the next, she could see the country thriving again.

"We're only seven people," Lena said. "Actually, six. One of ours is outside with our belongings."

"Six more people who can fight." Colin looked at Astrid. "And have done this before. She told me about that place out west."

The uprising at Glass House was different, Lena thought.

"How many do you have? Fighters? How many does Ivan have?" Beattie asked. "We're not getting involved in something that will fail."

"Mostly Ivan holds power because people are scared. We've got the old council behind us, and maybe twenty people. I'm counting on others jumping in on our side when we show them it's a winnable fight."

"We need to talk to the old council," Lena said, "and Beattie needs far more detail about your capabilities. Are you planning on letting your customers just get caught in the middle?"

"See, that's why we need you. Your questions get to the point. Most of the clients are back in their camp or room after curfew," Colin said. "We'll make sure there's a safe passage at the start, but we can't guarantee no one will get hurt if they jump in. We won't lose the fight over a few bruises and cuts."

That was something he'd have to deal with after it was over. Lena wasn't sure how the possibility of getting killed in a rebellion would affect their ability to reopen a market. And thinking the injuries would be so minor was callous.

"The council?" she asked. "I'll talk to them now. We aren't committing until I'm more comfortable that you might win."

48

"I can take you to them," Colin said. "We have another place like this."

How many hidden places existed inside Liberty?

"Are you sure Ivan doesn't know about this?" Beattie asked. "He was a smuggler, right? Hidden rooms would be valuable to him."

"He wasn't big time. We've dug up some information on him. All his traffic was in and out, no need to stash anything that could be found and confiscated. Now, he doesn't need to hide anything."

"Lena asked you a question," Astrid said. "You're acting all suspicious."

"The council can't get together much because Ivan keeps an eye on them. I can introduce you to three without a problem, if it's urgent. One is serving in Ivan's saloon, one is working a meat pie stand, and the other is in the stables."

"How many are there altogether?" Lena asked. Three out of six was one thing. Three out of twenty was too low to rely on what they had to say.

"Nine," Astrid answered. "I know where they all are and when the fighting starts, they are all ready."

"How do you know?" Beattie asked.

"Don't worry, I didn't give anything away. I mostly just watched them. They're all alert, like waiting for someone to set off a signal. I don't think they'll be much help in a fight, though. They are all pretty old."

This was just wasting time. Lena didn't need to get every answer. Astrid had gotten them stuck right in the middle of this... whatever it was. Knowing a fight was coming, she recognized the tension. It had been the same way at Glass House. She just didn't know it then. It was like everyone was holding their breath no matter who they supported. Ivan had to know it was coming. Maybe he didn't realize how soon, but the surprise wouldn't last long.

"You have plans?" she asked Colin.

"Yes. Why?"

"Are they written down?"

"It's a risk, but yes. They're here." Colin pointed at the pile of dusty drop sheets in the corner.

"Beattie and Astrid will look through them while you take me to the council members. If we're stuck helping, then we do this right. Unless I'm mistaken, you don't have any professionals with you."

"A few of the guards that got booted out, but not soldiers."

"We'll refine these as fast as we can," Beattie said as she pulled out a stack of papers from under the sheets.

"We'll be back in an hour?" Lena looked at Colin for confirmation. He nodded. "That's enough time to figure out a workable solution and still meet Scott, Tik, and Luis."

Beattie spread the documents out on the floor. "We might need more time, but my gut tells me we don't have it."

"I have a way of spreading the news, but making big changes to the plan at the last minute isn't smart, right?" Colin asked.

"When it kicks off, it will be chaos. Positioning at the start and distribution of skills, and maybe the place we use, all that can make the difference." Beattie turned her attention to Astrid and the plans.

LENA FOLLOWED Colin to the meat pie stand and met an older woman who was sweating over a stew pot.

While she worked, they moved closer, and Colin whispered introductions. The woman didn't react. Colin pointed at the list of prices and murmured to Lena, "Ask her your questions and she'll find a way to answer."

Now that she was standing there, Lena found it hard to boil down her questions to a few that would give her what she needed. She glanced at the price list to keep up the pretense and pursed her lips as if she was considering the choices. What did she really need? A conversation would be better, but this was all she had.

"How did it happen?" she asked.

"Surprise," the woman said. "Didn't see it coming, had a handful of people with guns and ammo. Threatened my kids."

Not the first time in history a change of leadership happened that way, Lena thought. "Are you ready?"

"Yes, now buy something or go."

Colin stepped forward and ordered a chicken pie.

They walked toward the stables, sharing the snack. "Just so you know, I don't have any credits," Lena said. "We came back to spend the last of them when we thought we're getting out."

"Figured. No one hangs onto our scrip. We're meeting Mike in the stables. You'll probably get to ask more questions, but don't take too long." Colin popped the last bit of crust into his mouth.

The stables were quiet. At this time of day, people were shopping or selling. Or having a last drink with friends. In an hour, whoever planned to leave today would be checking their horses and heading out.

"Curfew isn't far off," Lena said. "We'll have to leave, right?"

"No, you just can't sleep anywhere comfortable if you don't have credits. We'll put you up in the war room. The least we can do."

The very least. Lena had no desire to become a mercenary, so she'd settle for a roof and a meal or two until this was over.

"Colin." A man limped over to them. "You suddenly get a horse?"

"This is the woman we heard about," Colin said. "Is it safe to talk?"

"Never completely these days," Mike said. He drew them to an empty stall at the back. The horses on either side glanced their way, gave a quiet snort and then returned to their feedbags. "What do you want to know?"

"If we're going to get involved, I need to know we're not handing the place over to people who will be worse or will just lose it again."

"Nice. Look, we got caught not paying attention. It happened fast and vicious. He threatened bloodshed. If we'd noticed sooner, we'd have been ready to fight. Or, we would have gotten rid of the problem before he took over. You were here before, right?"

Lena nodded.

"Then you know Liberty wasn't perfect, but it was safe and honest. We'll bring it back. And we'll do a better job of defending it. If you got ideas on that, I'm listening."

Noise from the front of the stables caught his attention. "You got two more minutes before someone will come looking for me."

"How do you know it's the right time to fight?" Lena couldn't deny they were committed. Astrid had taken care of that with her impulsive offer. If she tried to take the others away now, someone would be tracking them down when this rebellion failed. And it would fail given the lack of detailed plans and the look on Beattie face when she saw the preparations.

"What will you do with the people following Ivan? And with Ivan, for that matter."

"Can't say we don't want to punish him before we hand out the death penalty. But we plan to come out of this as the good guys. He survives the fight, he goes in a cell. The people who followed him will be given a choice, leave and stay away, or work out some kind of community service repayment."

"Thanks," Lena said. She led Colin to the door. "I've heard enough."

49

Astrid and Beattie were sitting cross legged on the floor making notes on the original papers when Lena followed Colin into the war room. Astrid looked up as they entered. Colin bent to return the rolled-up fabric to the gap at the bottom of the door.

"How quickly can you get the changes out to your people?" Astrid asked without any hint at their progress.

"Ten or fifteen minutes," he said. "We have runners, and the place isn't that big."

"Does Ivan watch the fights?" Beattie asked.

"Usually." Colin leaned over and looked at the sketch and notes that had replaced the pages of planning. "Why?"

"Is there a schedule to the fights?" Beattie asked.

"One midday and one just before curfew. People can get some bets in and still be out before sunset. Why?"

"Is there one today?" Beattie asked.

"Why?" Colin asked again. "I need more than this to tell you what you need to know. Just answering questions will take too long."

"Best time to hit him will be during a fight," Lena said.

"They're planning to fill the audience with your people. Get Ivan trapped fast and put down the resistance. Like he did to you. Surprise, and this time not just threats of violence."

"A big crowd takes away the advantage of guns," Astrid said. "Even if they have bullets, numbers beat them. Will his fake council be there?"

"Usually," Colin said. "I don't know if they'll protect him or run."

Lena looked at her watch. If Colin was accurate about the timing, a fight would happen in less than an hour. Too soon to prepare, but the evening one would work. Anyone wanting out would be able to leave before someone tried to lock the gates.

"We are meeting three more of our group in the tavern near the fighting ring," Lena said. "We can check out the details as we walk though."

"Are you planning to start it during the noon fight?" Colin asked.

"No, we'll look for proof our plan will work," Astrid said. "Then you can send out the instructions. We'll do it tonight."

"Now it's set in motion, we can't wait long," Beattie said. "Enough people will have to know so we'll have fighters. That means there's a risk someone on Ivan's side will hear the preparations and our plan will fall apart."

"Tonight works," Colin said. "We need to spread the news in the next few minutes."

The walk through the center of the market gave Lena enough assurance that they could choke the entrances with only a few people and keep the turmoil from destroying Liberty. She noticed the bleachers weren't set up. "When are the stands pulled out?"

"When the crowd almost fills the open space," Colin said. "Ivan's people don't like to work if they can avoid it."

They took a table in the back of the tavern, ordering enough food and drink to assure they weren't disturbed. The place wasn't large. Mainly a front door, a bar that ran along the right wall and a few tables in the narrow space between the bar and left wall. In the back, a swinging door led to a kitchen. The aroma was comforting. Warm stewed meat and herbs, bread, and something fruity.

Colin told the waitress to add whatever they ordered to his tab. "I'll get reimbursed when we win," he said when they were alone.

Tik and Scott joined them a few minutes later. "Luis is just behind us," Scott said. "Everything is settled with Mellow."

Their food arrived and Lena thanked the waitress. Astrid introduced Colin and they dug in. Lena, sitting with her back to the wall, kept her eye on the door. Two other tables were occupied and none of the guests were paying them any attention.

"How will you get the news out?" she asked. "We don't have a lot of time."

"Give me the details. I'll go and find our runners."

"Don't come back," Beattie said. "It will bring attention."

"Then start talking," Colin said.

Beattie glanced at Astrid and then gave a small nod.

"There are only four ways into the fight ring," Astrid said. "The vendor stalls are doing a great job of blocking off anything else. We need people to start filling the space and only letting in your allies. How early do people usually get there?"

"Only in the last half hour," Colin said. "I can get thirty

people, not enough for an entire audience though. If the bleachers go up, will your plan still work?"

"Blocking access is the most important," Beattie said. "Can someone disable the mechanism that moves the stand?"

"Probably," Colin said. "It's shoddy work. We'll make sure it happens."

Luis joined them before Beattie could tell more details.

"My buddies left this morning. Not a good sign."

Astrid gave everyone a summary of the plan. "Your friends have good timing," she said at the end.

"How the hell did we get here so close to the fight?" Luis asked.

"Your getting here gave us confidence," Colin said. "No one travels with soldiers these days. Maybe that's coming, but not yet."

Lena found herself wondering if Tik's idea of a band of peacekeepers would help speed up travel. If people could hire protection, would the gangs give up on the idea of attacking anyone on the road or would they just band together for strength? The people traffickers were not the only gang operating along their route. Like everyone else, small gangs tended to stay in their territory.

"Will everyone be able to bring weapons they can hide?" Tik asked. "No way will anyone let a bunch of armed people hang out together."

"We don't have big weapons," Colin said. "Is there anything else I need to tell the runners?"

"No, we'll see you tonight." Astrid turned to the food and grabbed a slice of bread covered with melted cheese.

"We can't stay in here all day," Beattie said. "If we don't get into position early, the fight will be out of control. Okay, more out of control. I need to observe the setup, make a few adjustments in real time."

Lena hated the idea of hiding until the last minute, too, but Ivan knew her and Astrid. If he saw them, it could throw everything off. "We need disguises," she said.

Astrid looked up from where she was arranging the empty plates and dishes. "Why?"

"I wish I'd done this before we arrived," Lena said. "Ivan might recognize you and me. What do you think he'll do when he runs into the girl who escaped, and the woman who was looking for her?"

"Luis was searching for me, too," Astrid said.

"I'm just another guy," Luis said. "You stand out in your Vikingness. Lena's right. We've taken a foolish risk."

"I'm not going to be sent away," Astrid said. "You need me in this fight."

"We know," Lena said. "I'm not talking about putting you in a dress. You need to hide your hair, and try to be less... I don't know, confident, until we start fighting. I'll wear a scarf."

"We don't have one," Astrid said.

"Stop arguing," Beattie said. "I'll find two scarves big enough to let you both pass as someone harmless. I have a few things I can trade. You both wait here for the five minutes it will take." Beattie slipped away without letting Astrid argue any further.

"He hasn't noticed me yet," Astrid said.

Her pout had nothing to do with hiding, Lena thought. Astrid wanted Ivan to recognize her and know she was the one who brought him down. She couldn't blame the girl, but it didn't change the fact that it would blow the whole plan if he saw her too soon.

"He might not have seen you," Luis said. "We haven't

been there for the fights. He doesn't walk around and give people a chance to express their distaste for his regime."

The waitress came past to clear the empty plates and hinted that the table would be needed. The tavern was starting to fill up the closer they got to the time for the first fight of the day. Lena was as anxious as the others to get an idea of the challenges they'd face. If the regular crowd was usually half-drunk, it would pose danger they needed to mitigate.

The door opened and Beattie came back to the table. She didn't have any disguises.

"We're too late," she said. "It's already started."

L ena stepped out into the hard, spring sunshine hoping Beattie was wrong. What should have been a crowd of people reacting to two fighters in the ring was a melee of individual battles. Lena couldn't see any difference between the combatants. No evidence of good guy or bad guy.

The noise of flesh smacking into flesh, grunts of pain and shouts of rage pushed against her. "What the hell happened?" she asked, leaning in toward Beattie.

"I didn't see it start," she said. "I heard someone shouting and then a scream. If this isn't the rebellion, it's going to do enough damage to rip this place apart."

Her whole group was pinned against the tavern wall as people stumbled into them or were pushed. "Okay, what do we do?"

"We split up. You have weapons on you?"

"We all do," Lena said. "How do we know who to fight?"

"You don't," Astrid said. "Just fight your way through. We need to get people in here to create the sides we need. It doesn't matter what started it."

Beattie instructed everyone to get into pairs and make their way to the other side, toward the stables. They were to regroup and find Colin. While she talked, the fighting got wilder as people from the market joined. A stall was toppled to Lena's right. Scott grabbed her arm and steered her to the fringes of the grappling bodies.

"Don't get separated from me," he said in her ear. "Get your knife out. Try not to make things worse. I'm not sure that's possible, but try."

She jammed her body next to his as they moved.

Lena pulled Scott to stop as they almost stumbled into a pair of women. One kicked her opponent, then grabbed her braid to drag her out of the melee.

As she took a step forward, a man elbowed Lena, knocking her away from Scott's side. She shoved the fighter into the fists of a guard. The guard's gun was stretched away as someone tried to steal it.

The stink of sweat and blood thickened the air. Lena repressed her gag and looked for Scott.

He was a few paces ahead of her. She grabbed his arm and pulled herself back to his side.

She glanced over to the center of the square when a child screamed. Two kids of about five were standing in the ring, crying. Another joined them as someone tossed her to safety.

Scott was pulled away again by another guard. He hit the man on the temple with the grip of his knife, and she tore his gun away. The weapon was no use in this tangle of fists and elbows, but having one gave Lena a sense of power.

A hand grabbed a fistful of her hair. She turned with her blade ready to slice at the attacker. The sight of Colin ahead distracted her long enough for the attacker to pull her backward.

Swinging her knife in the direction of the tug, she connected with the man's arm. Her hair was freed and the attacker stood cursing, trying to stem the flow of blood.

Scott grabbed her other hand to stop the sheer press of bodies pushing them apart.

"Colin is over there," Lena hissed.

"I know. He's waiting for us and directing his people into the fight."

Every step toward the man was a struggle. Twice Lena had to hold onto Scott to avoid falling when a stray kick connected with her rather than the intended victim. Scott deflected punches to keep them moving forward.

And suddenly they were through. Not out of the fighting, but on the edge where they could gain some distance from the wild flailing.

A steady stream of people ran toward the battle, most of them directed by Colin. Far more than the thirty he'd promised. The chaos seemed to form sides, but immediately shifted back to individual groups.

"Where is Ivan?" Scott said.

"Trying to get out," Colin said and pointed with his chin to the far side of the battle. "He'd be better off using his guards to beat this down, but he's more interested in getting safe than taking back order."

Lena tested the stability of the closest stall. She stood on the counter to get a better view. "It's not working," she said. "The fights keep surging around him and blocking his way. Despite it looking like a riot, there is some thought to the targets."

"It took a bit for our people to get here," Colin said. "That's what you're seeing now. They are trying to get to him or keep him in danger."

"Can you see the others?" Scott asked.

"Beattie and Astrid are close to Ivan," she said. "I can't see Tik or Luis."

"Anyone down or badly hurt?" Colin asked. "Can you tell from here?"

"It looks like significant bruises and a few scratches so far," Lena said. "Most people only have their hands to use as weapons. There's a few knives, but not enough room for anyone to do much damage."

"It won't last long," Scott said. "This is burning too hot to last."

"We need to get in there and help," Colin said.

A bloody combatant stumbled free and collapsed a few steps into the aisle. A rock followed. Someone had found new weapons.

"No," Lena said. "We don't need another fighter. Someone must be ready to call for order when the energy bleeds out."

"I can't just stand here," Colin said. "What if the guards recover and start shooting?"

"And if you die, how will anyone restore Liberty?" Lena asked. She knew the feeling from the battle for the farm. Watching people you knew and loved going into battle while you waited to fulfill your role was impossible. She hadn't managed it, but Colin would have to. "Where are the other council members?"

"They were supposed to go to the war room to be safe. I'm pretty sure not all of them did. I'm here, so I can't blame them."

"How did it start?" Scott asked.

"Ivan was trying to make kids fight," Colin said. "Two women protested. Two thugs didn't like it. Ivan told his guards to take the women away. A stall owner stepped forward to protect them. Another joined in. The thugs started fighting. The guards were caught by surprise and the next second, it was like this."

"That's what you'll use to calm it," Scott said. "The kids are safe. So let the fighters keep it up until they are too exhausted. Then get their attention."

"Where are you going?" Lena asked.

"In to help," Scott said. "You stay here to protect him. I'll find Tik and Luis."

51

A couple of minutes later, the sounds turned from grunts and shouts to screams. She nudged Colin a few steps back toward the open spaces, wishing she could climb back onto the stall to see what triggered the sudden intensity.

"We need information," Colin said. "I'll stay out of it, I promise. You need to know what's happening."

Since when did her job include General? Lena told Colin to stay just on the edge, and if the fight surged toward him, to run to the war room. He nodded and took a step back as if to prove he'd heard.

The crowd was still pushing outward, not yet fleeing, but something over to the right of the arena was demanding space.

Lena climbed onto the counter and looked over the heads of the observers.

Her eyes first went to the fighting ring. The space contained about ten kids of various ages. The older ones stood between the mob and the younger ones. She didn't need to think where the kids came from. A lot of the vendors ran their stalls as family businesses. Kids worked alongside grandparents.

Another scream came from the widening gap to the side.

Scott and Tik jumped into the ring to protect the kids. Tik wiped blood from his eyes, but Lena couldn't see any wound. Scott wasn't hurt, but his shirt had a rip in the shoulder seam.

She scanned the gap where the screams had come from only a minute before.

Beattie was clearing people away from a fight in the center, blood dripping from her long knife. Luis was helping her drag unconscious fighters away.

There was no sight of a guard. More accurately, there was no sign of anyone trying to stop what was happening.

Astrid balanced from foot to foot, grinning, her braids tipped with blood, her knives held ready to slash.

A chant started quietly, then got louder as it was picked up by more voices, spreading through the crowd like a wave.

"Kill him. Kill him."

Colin touched Lena's foot to get her attention. "Is it safe for me up there, too?"

"I don't know, but you need to see what's happening, right?"

Colin leaned on the counter, and it didn't move or creak. Lena reached down and helped him to join her. It was tight. She leaned into him so they took less space and still had a view of the action.

"Astrid," Colin said. "Not a surprise."

"You see any guards?" Lena asked, trying to check her assumptions.

Colin looked around the mass of people. "No. They were mostly hired thugs. I guess the risk of not getting paid got too much for them."

The chant continued, and it became difficult to hear anything but the demand for retribution.

This was the moment for Astrid to take her revenge. The crowd wanted the same thing. Killing in defense of someone was very different from the execution Lena feared was coming. That kind of action stayed with you forever.

"Can you see who it is?" Lena asked Colin.

"Ivan? Who else would it be?" Colin shifted his weight, and the counter moved under their feet. They both tensed but the structure held.

"We need to be sure," Lena said.

"There's no time to join them," Colin said. "Too many people in the way."

"Stand up!" Astrid shouted at her opponent. "Fight."

The chant died.

When there was no response, Astrid stuck one of her knives into the ground and reached forward. She pulled Ivan to stand opposite her. He staggered at the force of her effort, but from where Lena stood, she couldn't see any injuries.

"Now we know," Colin said, his voice loud in the silence.

"I wish we weren't relying on her good judgment," Lena said. "You don't want to start over with the stain of an execution."

"Maybe in the old world, that made sense. When there was a justice system," Colin said. "Things are different now."

Lena agreed with him, but not that it was only the old world. Justice didn't need an overloaded court system to be fair. This situation wasn't unique. The problem came when she tried to convince people unity was valuable without a battle to emphasize the point.

"Fight!" Astrid all but screamed.

Ivan put his hands in the air.

Beattie and Luis stepped behind Astrid, but from Lena's vantage point, she couldn't see if either gave the girl advice.

Astrid pulled her knife from the ground, wiped it on her jeans and stuck it back in its sheathe. Still holding the other, she shifted her grip from fighting to simply holding. Relief drained Lena's energy. The old Astrid would never have withdrawn from an opportunity to avenge a wrong.

The girl turned her attention to the crowd. "Go home. This is over. I will not dishonor my family by killing a prisoner."

No one moved.

"I will not let you kill him either," she said. "Go home. Take your children to safety. Apologize to the people you injured. Tomorrow, it all starts new."

The people at the fringes shuffled away, the ones closer to Ivan took longer to move. Some needed to be pulled away by friends or partners.

"Go to the other merchants," Lena said. "You need to take control fast. We'll clean up here."

Like the others, Colin didn't move right away. Then he mumbled something she didn't catch before jumping to the ground and walking away.

Lena checked to make sure Ivan was being guarded and protected from anyone less principled than Astrid.

She jumped down and walked toward the prisoner. Scott and Tik helped the last of the kids down and started encouraging people to disperse faster.

By the time Lena joined the small group, the square containing the arena was empty. In the background, she heard sounds of stalls being opened and a few vendors calling out their wares.

"What happened?" she asked as she stepped beside Astrid.

"He was escaping," Astrid said. "We were going to grab him, tie him up for dealing with later. But he stabbed a guard."

"The guard was trying to run," Beattie said. "He waited too long."

That explained the blood soaking into the ground. "Is he getting help?"

"No. He's dead. The body got dragged away." Astrid wiped her second blade and sheathed it. "Ivan should have fought me."

"I'm not stupid," Ivan said. "This way, I get to live. Maybe I'll be banished. I have people I can go to."

"And you planned to bring back an army?" Tik asked. "Don't count on the council being quite so bound by rules about killing. If they think you are a threat, they could decide to shut it down permanently."

"We'll take him," a woman said. She was accompanied by two men with shackles. "Hated that he let stuff like this into the market, but it comes in handy now."

"Where are you taking him?" Lena wasn't going to let Ivan out of her sight until he was in a cell.

"To jail," Mike, the council member who'd worked in the stables, said as he strode across the open space. "We're going to deal with him. You don't need to be involved. There's a meeting for the whole market at dusk. We're moving all remaining visitors outside for the night, but you can stay."

"We need to get cleaned up," Lena said, "and inform the person waiting at our camp."

"Be back before the doors close," Mike said. "We'll adjust the curfew later, but for today, it's safer for us to mete out justice without outsiders."

"I'll go," Luis said. "I don't need to be here for the meeting. We'll see you tomorrow."

52

The council put them up in a hotel. With all the visitors outside the walls, there was plenty of accommodations. As they crossed the market, Lena noticed it was back to business even before the battleground was cleared. But only the locals were shopping, and perhaps they were doing more gossiping than purchasing.

She was relieved to find none of her people were injured beyond bruises and a couple of scrapes, once they were cleaned up. Mostly they were in shock and dealing with the adrenalin flooding their systems.

"I'll feel better when we're on the road," Scott said. "This place is going to be on the boiling point for a while. The council has its hands full proving they can do the job this time."

"It starts with how they punish Ivan," Lena said. "Do that right and people will just go back about their business."

"Maybe we'll head out after this meeting," Tik said.

"I'm sure we can convince them to let us go when we want," Beattie said. "They might actually kick us out."

Astrid looked up from her braids. She'd undone them to

clean the blood and was putting them all back together with Beattie's help. "But we saved them."

"That doesn't mean anything when the fight is over," Beattie said. "Now we're just the people who were bad enough to get rid of the problem, and potentially become the next problem."

"So, we can't come back?" Astrid asked. "Not that we're planning on leaving the farm for a while, but this is a market."

"They just need distance," Lena said. "Let's see what happens at the meeting. Bring everything with you in case we don't want to risk coming back to the room."

A few hours later, Lena walked back into the open square. The ropes were gone from the ring, and now it was simply a stage. A table and chairs waited in the middle of the raised floor. One chair faced the nine behind the table.

People were already gathering, eager for the final step in getting their market back.

"You're still here." Anne, the woman from Beta, was standing beside them.

"I thought all visitors were sent outside," Tik said.

"My group disappeared on me yesterday," Anne said. "I'm headed to the gates now. Just saw you and thought I'd say hi."

"Why would your group leave without you?" Lena asked.

"They weren't really my group," Anne said. "I'm just information seeking for Beta. I joined up with a party halfway here. I guess they didn't feel responsible for me. I'll be walking back alone."

A guard came by and told Anne to keep moving toward the gate.

"I'll camp outside tonight," she said with a wave. "Maybe I'll see you again on the road."

A boy ran up to them and stopped in front of Astrid, a look of hero worship glowing on his face. "The council wants all of you on the stage. Come with me, please."

Astrid straightened up at his words. Lena hoped she wouldn't be disappointed by reality. The council might be thanking them, or asking for advice on punishments, or ordering them to leave. Or, worst of all, asking them to leave and take Ivan with them.

She followed the child to a set of steps that had been erected in the last couple of hours. Once on the stage, the crowd cheered. That could mean anything, too.

Colin and the other eight council members walked onto the stage. When they were seated, Colin beckoned them closer.

"The meeting will start in ten minutes or so," he said. "We'll light torches and then tell people what the future will be. I want you here to thank you, so everyone knows you have our support and are welcome. We'll bring Ivan up and pronounce his sentence. There's a town hall after that, gives people the opportunity voice concerns rather than stew on them."

"When do you want us to leave?" Beattie asked.

"Before the town hall," Colin said. "You can stay in the rooms until tomorrow. You are welcome to stay and listen to the conversation, but you are not part of our community."

"I don't like leaving Mellow and Luis out there alone," Tik said. "Too many people on the road since you kicked out your clients."

"I understand. We have payment, or you can think of them as gifts, if you like. Can we come to your camp tomorrow morning?"

They wouldn't be moving on until light, anyway. And a day's rest wouldn't make the difference in the long journey home. "Sure, we'll be leaving by midday, but come see us before that."

Colin checked to make sure he was clear about their location, and then torches flared to light.

The ceremony was short. Colin spoke for the council. He thanked them, and the crowd cheered again.

Ivan was brought to the stage by the same people who'd taken him into custody. They chained him to the single chair. It was mostly for show because nothing stopped him from pulling free. Except his shackles would trip him on the first step.

"You are facing multiple charges," Colin said loud enough to carry to the audience. "You led an uprising against the leaders of this community with outside forces. Your crimes while in power are too many to list. And your final act was murder."

Ivan shrugged.

"We have discussed your punishment. We cannot allow you to go free and bring another brutal force to bear. The risk you will find a way to escape is too high to keep you in jail for your life."

He was drawing out the announcement. Lena tried to think how she might handle it. His death took away all the risks, but it also set a pall over the new community.

"We do not wish to start rebuilding Liberty on your blood. That is your way, not ours. Our conclusion is that we will exile you. You will be escorted east until a suitable place is found. We will provide you with food and equipment to survive for a week. If you return to Liberty alone or with a force, you will be executed."

"Only if you catch me," Ivan said. He turned to glare at Lena. "You won't feel so smug when my partners get to your little home. They have long memories."

"Are they planning to head our way?" Astrid asked as she touched the hilt of her knife.

Ivan spat on the canvas. "They will when I tell them about you."

"Enough," Colin snapped. "To warn other communities, we will also tattoo your crime on your forehead."

Colin indicated to the guards to take him away. Ivan struggled against their hold.

"You might as well kill me fast," he shouted. "I can't survive out there alone."

"Many people do," Colin said.

The crowd was shocked into silence for a long beat, as if expecting a more final result. Something to satisfy the revenge they craved.

53

W hen they got to their camp, Anne was chatting with Luis and Mellow. As much as Lena wanted to talk over the events and the impact on everyone, Anne's presence meant any private discussion would have to wait.

"I figured we'd want to make sure of her," Luis said to Lena as he helped take the saddle off Bebop. "Lots of people on the road, so we need to keep alert. And I didn't want to leave her to be attacked."

"Some people aren't satisfied with the result," Tik said as they joined Mellow and Anne around the fire.

"Did you tell Mellow about the fight?" Lena asked.

"Told them both," Luis said. "What happened later?"

"Okay. The council will be here in the morning." Lena looked around to make sure no one was camping close. "Let's settle in and we'll figure out our next moves."

It was early enough in the day to move on, but she'd promised Colin they could meet. It would be good to hear what he had to say. They'd dealt with Ivan fairly, but right now she'd be happy never seeing Liberty again. Both times they'd stopped had been dangerous. First, Astrid was taken, and then a violent rebellion. To be fair, the catalyst for both was gone, but bad people seemed to be the only ones in power, and she didn't know the new or old council well enough.

"Did they say which way he was going?" Mellow asked after Lena told them about the punishment.

"East," Astrid said. "I talked to Colin about that. We can't let them deliver him to his gang friends back there. So, they'll leave him in the mountains. Safe, but isolated."

"How do you feel about that?" Mellow asked.

"You mean, do I want to hunt him down and kill him slowly?" She grinned like that was exactly her plan.

"Something like that," Mellow said.

"He was Liberty's problem and he's going to learn what it's like to try to survive alone. Really survive. I'll sleep well."

"That's the kind of thing Da Vinci would do," Anne said. She'd been quiet since Lena arrived, just watching everyone.

"Are you headed back to Beta?" Luis asked. "Report on what you've seen?"

"I'm supposed to be exploring. Liberty was my first big community. Is it all like that?"

"Why did Da Vinci send you alone?" Lena asked. "That seems risky."

"I could be spared," Anne said. "He made a big step forward on power supplies. I came with a couple of others, but the road is dangerous." Her voice cracked on the last part, and she didn't expand.

"And she's on foot," Luis said. "It's going to take her a long time to get home."

Lena didn't want to invite Anne to join them without checking with the others. It was going to be difficult to get private time for the discussion. It was time she didn't want to spend after Colin's visit. "Maybe we can get you some supplies from Liberty tomorrow. They want to pay us, and right now they'll be feeling generous."

BY NIGHTFALL, everyone was drooping. Lena set short watches. It was her only time to talk to each of her friends and, despite the exhaustion, she didn't expect anyone to get a full eight hours of sleep.

Anne offered to take a shift, but Lena declined. It didn't matter if she was the safest person they would meet, Lena wouldn't give her the opportunity to steal their supplies or kill them.

By morning, she had her answer about adding Anne. No one was willing to let her travel alone. Scott's words settled the uneasiness Lena hadn't been able to name. "Be Bozeman, not Crouch. How will you feel if something happens to her?"

"So, invite her to travel with us, but don't just close our eyes to the risk." That approach felt more like the world she'd wanted to create a year ago in the farmhouse kitchen.

"We'll need another horse at some point," Luis said. "Liberty might be our best bet."

The horses nickered and shifted. Lena tensed. In the daylight it wouldn't be other animals causing them concern.

54

"It's Colin," Tik said from his position next to the road. "And two others. Three spare horses."

"Break the camp," Lena said. "I want to be traveling as soon as we're done."

"Morning," Colin said.

"How are things back there?" Mellow asked. "Is the clinic able to manage?"

If Mellow offered her services, they would be delayed for days. Lena wouldn't deny her if it came to that, but she wanted to be on the road and away from the memories of yesterday.

Colin thanked her for the offer but said there was no need. "The great thing about merchants is they bounce back if there's a profit to be made. Most of the clients came back this morning. We'll be fine."

"Good to hear," Luis said. "Should we get down to it? Unlike your other customers, we're happy to head out."

Colin dismounted and indicated for his guards to join him. "I brought a selection of goods," he said. "Let's find a common price quickly."

Lena invited Colin and his escort to join them at the remnants of the fire they'd kept going through the night. Colin declined the offer of tea and suggested the others in the group look through the bags. In moments, Lena and Luis were alone with Colin. A better mix for negotiating.

"I'll start," Colin said. "Normally I wouldn't, but your services were unusual, and I hope we never come to a point when we have a standard fee for protecting the market. One of the horses and half the bags. They contain food and trade items to get you on your way."

Lena glanced at Luis. She would have been happy with the first offer. It gave Anne a horse, and they'd be able to get home without stopping for supplies. Luis took over, as they'd agreed before Colin arrived.

"You should have brought less," he said. "You've got all three horses weighed down. Our pack horse is already laden. We'll take two horses, all the food, and whatever of the trade goods we decide will be useful."

"I can spare two of the horses," Colin said. "I need at least one to bring back what you don't take. Half the food and half of the supplies."

Lena tuned out the discussion, trusting Luis to get the best deal. She glanced at the activity around the horses. Packs were on the ground, some opened, others put to the side. She realized Beattie was organizing them. And at closer inspection, it became clear Anne was standing close to one pile, Scott to another. They were signaling to Luis what he should bargain for — smart.

"Lena." Colin's voice broke through her thoughts.

"We're done?" she asked.

"I would like to speak to you alone, if possible. I have some information you may not wish to share at first."

"We don't keep secrets," Lena said.

"I meant more like you may want to digest it before talking to your companions."

"Is it about Anne?"

"No. I see she joined you, but that is not something I would know how to advise you on."

Luis had gone to join the rest of the group in packing their new bags. Two horses were separated from the group, Anne holding their reins. Both were saddled and wearing full tack. Luis was adding bags to them, and Scott led their pack horse over so they could balance the load.

"We're as alone as we will be," she said.

"Are you still looking for communities to link together?"

"It's been fruitless up to now, but why are you asking?" Is he about to offer an alliance with Liberty? Lena did her best to keep the question from showing on her face.

"It is in Liberty's interest to have safe travel, and your vision will make it happen, eventually. I've heard about a community, not exactly on your way home, but it is thriving and would make a good partner."

Was she ready for one more disappointment? "Tell me what you know, and I'll ask my friends if they are interested. If we find anything of value, we'll send a message to you somehow."

"It's called Haven. In old Chicago. They've been taking people in since the end of the plagues. It's stable and well managed."

"How do you know about it?" Lena asked. "Chicago is a long way from here. I'm surprised anyone comes that far to trade."

The activity off to the side was slowing down. The camp was ready to move on.

"We're hoping to attract a wider customer base," Colin

said. "My information isn't firsthand. People talk. I guess word is spreading, and we should start planning a few more locations when things settle. But people I trust believe the stories. I will leave it with you." He stood and beckoned the guards to join him.

"We need to decide on this Haven thing soon," Scott said as they looked over the maps.

"I know," Lena said. "But I don't want to sit here all day. When is our turn off?"

"We can still go off the road at any point," Scott said, indicating the smaller routes on the map. "Two days from now, if we're taking our time. If we can decide fast, tomorrow is the first clear off ramp."

"We can talk and ride," Mellow said. "Make the decision when we stop for a rest. We aren't going to get any more information than what's in front of us now, so it shouldn't be hard."

Lena agreed and took one last look at the map. Chicago was a long way from home. The days would get brighter, and they could ride farther as they got south, but it was going to be almost three months to get there. Twice as long as it would take to get home. And then coming back would be a month if nothing went wrong. Summer would be more than half over by the time they were back at the farm.

If the journey gave them something important, time

didn't really matter. If this Haven place was what Colin thought, it meant there was hope, not for a coast-to-coast unity, but a wider collection of allies on their side of the world.

If it was a threat, a month's travel was too close to be ignorant of the danger. If it turned out to be anything else, it didn't matter.

By the time they settled for the night in a rest area. this one was not empty but populated with a handful of small groups, Lena was still turning options over in her mind. Ignoring this Haven would leave her worried about it at home. Going could expose the farm to danger.

Luis and Anne settled the horses just beside the spot they'd chosen to camp. Their reins looped over tree branches to keep them from wandering. Food and water in buckets half buried in the dirt to keep them from being knocked over. Their supplies piled between the animals and the fire.

"Can I help with dinner?" Anne asked as she returned from the makeshift paddock.

"Sure," Lena said. "See if you can find a few dry branches while I get the fire started."

"I'll come with you," Beattie said. "I want the fire on all night because we're going to keep a close guard on our stuff. It's been a while since we had to share a camp."

More than a while, Lena thought. They'd never shared the night with strangers around them. Another reminder of how empty the world was of humans now. If Liberty hadn't boiled over into a riot, their camp mates would likely be still in the market, or much farther along their journey because they'd delayed to see the results of the riot.

When the two women were out of earshot, Luis joined her at the fire. "You want to talk plans in front of Anne?"

"We don't have a choice," Lena said. "I'm not sending her away, and maybe she has a perspective on this we won't see."

He reached in and lit the tinder before speaking again. "I guess we're equipped to keep an eye on her. And most of us have made our decisions anyway. We need to keep the details of home out of the discussion."

"You don't trust her?"

"I'm not the only one. She's keeping something secret. It could be nothing to do with us, but her being alone doesn't sit right."

"It's been a while since anyone joined us," Lena said. "We'll stay alert. Let's get those cans of stew from Liberty in the pot."

The rest area quieted soon after the sun went down. No one was camping close to any other fire, so they had enough privacy to talk without giving away their plans.

They set the guard schedule, more than just a watch for danger since they had so much to protect. Two people always awake. One with the horses and one with the humans. No one would be sleeping easily for a while.

"Okay, so decision time," Lena said after the dinner dishes were cleaned. "Let's get all the issues out first before anyone voices their decision."

"I want to go," Astrid said as if Lena hadn't spoken. "I think we should know. At least as far as looking at the place. Like we've done before."

"You can't always tell from observing," Anne said. "I know I don't have a vote, and you've all been on the road longer than me. If it's bad, how do know without getting caught up in whatever's going on?"

"We've known in the past," Astrid said. "Yeah, not every time, but there have to be communities closer who know what's happening at this Haven."

"If this is really in Chicago, they had a lot of parks," Luis said. "Most people know it as a downtown with no greenery and lots of tall buildings. It's not the full picture. They could be growing their own food."

"Or using some of the outlying areas for farms," Scott said. "We can't judge every city by Portland. Or Glass House, or Crouch. Okay, I'll stop now."

"We haven't been to any other city." Lena pointed out. "Mostly we've bypassed them. For a reason."

"You don't want to look?" Mellow asked. "What about your big dream of unity?"

It had been drained out of her by experience. Was that really true? She'd been so certain last year that it was possible. Was one more try really so useless?

"I think we should vote," Beattie said. "I think we at least look around the area."

"Me too," Astrid said. "It's stupid not to go. Unless you plan to do this again? Travel around looking for allies?"

"We agree," Mellow said. "Tik and I decided earlier. We are going to look even if you head home."

"Whatever you decide," Scott said. "I think we should go, but I'm not forcing it."

"I'm interested in seeing what's going on in the east," Luis said. "I've traveled alone enough to take care of myself or go with Mellow and Tik."

The thought of splitting up gave Lena chills. It sounded like Scott and Lena would be heading to the farm alone if that was what she decided. She'd pictured them all riding up to the porch and surprising everyone.

"I think Da Vinci would want me to go," Anne said. "So, I'm hoping I can tag along with whoever heads to Chicago."

"So, we all go," Lena said. "I don't want to miss out on all the fun."

WANT MORE

~

Will Lena and her friends find a partner in Chicago to start civilization again? Find out by grabbing your copy of THE HAVEN.

~

If you enjoyed reading THE GLASS HOUSE please

consider helping other readers to find the story by leaving a review.

FREE BOOK

Claim your copy of A Choice to Make when you sign up for my newsletter and get a glimpse of Lena and Brian at the end of the plagues.

ALSO BY P A WILSON

For more books by P A Wilson or Poppy Bridgeman
scan the QR code below or go to pawilson.ca

ABOUT P A WILSON

Perry Wilson is a Canadian author based in Vancouver, BC who has big ideas and an itch to tell stories. Having spent some time on university, a career, and life in general, she returned to writing in 2008 and hasn't looked back since (well, maybe a little, but only while parallel parking).

She is a member of the Vancouver Writers Social Group, The Royal City Literary Arts Society, and The Surrey Writing Workshop. Perry has self-published several novels. She writes the Madeline Journeys, a fantasy series about a high-powered lawyer who finds herself trapped in a magical world, the Quinn Larson Quests, which follows the adventures of a wizard named Quinn who must contend with volatile fae in the heart of Vancouver, and the Charity Deacon Investigations, a mystery thriller series about a private eye who tends to fall into serious trouble with her cases, and The Riverton Romances, a series based in a small town in Oregon, one of her favorite states. Her stand-alone novels are Breaking the Bonds, Closing the Circle, and The Dragon at The Edge of The Map.

For more information
www.pawilson.ca
pawilson@pawilson.ca

ACKNOWLEDGMENTS

People think that the process of writing is solitary. That's not the case for me. I have help from so many people it would be hard to acknowledge everyone, but I'll give it a try.

The support and inspiration I get from my writer's groups is incalculable. The Vancouver Writers Social Group opens my mind to other ways of telling a story. The Royal City Literary Arts Society gives me the opportunity to meet and share with other writers who have more knowledge than I do. The Other 11 Months group is where I learn about getting the words on the page. And my critique group who helps me find the best parts of the story I want to tell. Thanks to all of the members of these great groups.

Last of all, but definitely a huge part of the process, my beta readers. These are the people who love stories and are willing, and more than able, to tell me if my finished story is ready for you, my readers.

www.ingramcontent.com/pod-product-compliance
Lightning Source LLC
Chambersburg PA
CBHW020312200626
46814CB00006BA/2204